DEDICATION

I'd like to dedicate this book to all those "Lizzies" out there who are struggling in their unique situations in school.

Most adults would agree that they would never want to relive those middle school years!

Please don't ever give up on yourself. God made you for a purpose and has a plan for your life. He loves you so much more than you can even imagine! Hang in there and pray often. You may be the only light in someone's life. Live your life well. The Lord knows your frustrations, so give your problems to him and he will help you through them. If you feel that life has become too much to bear, speak to a trusted, godly adult who can help you. Remember that this time in your life too, shall pass!

Rom. 8:28

ACKNOWLEDGEMENTS

I'd like to thank my wonderful husband Joel and daughter Kylee along with all of my family for your encouragement and support.

Thanks also to my dear sister and editor, Paula Seiffert for your endless hours of editing and great suggestions. Thank you to my always helpful son-in-law, Andy Elling for all of your technical help. I couldn't have done this without all of you!

A special thanks go out to my awesome illustrators, Pam Jones, Jenni Freytag and Kylee Gerken.

CHAPTER 1

SCHOOL DAZE!

"Be anxious for nothing..."

"Lizzy, it's time to get up. We leave in an hour," called Mom from the bedroom doorway.

"I'm awake, Mom," said Lizzy sleepily she sat up and stretched her arms.

"You have a big day today. Your first day of 6th grade. Are you excited?" Mom questioned lovingly.

"I guess so," replied Lizzy. "It'll be fun to see Jordan again. I wish she wouldn't have had to spend the whole summer at her dad's."

Lizzy had missed her best friend during the long summer months. Many times she didn't have any friends nearby to hang around with.

"I know, Honey," Mom agreed. "But it will be nice to catch up with her and find out what she did over the summer. You'll have to tell her all about your camping trip with your dad!"

"Yeah, I'll fill her in on everything!" promised Lizzy.

Suddenly Max, the family's Great Dane jumped onto Lizzy's bed and licked her on the mouth.

"Eww! Get down, Max!" scolded Lizzy as she pushed him away. She tasted the distinct flavor of Kibbles and Nibbles in her mouth. "I hope I don't have dog breath all day!" complained Lizzy.

"I'm planning on calling Golden Paws Obedience School today to find out what they charge for dog training," said Mom. "Max has gotten a little out of hand."

"That's for sure!" agreed Lizzy.

"Anyway, you should have a great day today," added Mom. "Just pay close attention to your teachers. It may be a little more challenging with switching classes, but it should make the day go faster."

"Yeah, I think so, too. I'm just afraid I'll go to the wrong room or do something embarrassing," moaned Lizzy.

"I'm sure you'll do just fine," assured Mom. "You have your schedule with the room numbers, and there will be a couple of teachers in the hallways to direct you if you need help. I'll say a prayer for you, too."

"Thanks, I'll need it," Lizzy responded.

Lizzy was almost too nervous to eat breakfast, but finally decided on a piece of cinnamon toast and a glass of milk. Her mom always knew what she liked and would cook her favorite foods. As Mom left the room to make her toast, Lizzy began to get ready for school. Lizzy had anticipated the start of the school year with mixed emotions. Last year had not been an easy year, due to her struggles with math and the constant teasing from some of her classmates. Lizzy was a sensitive, thoughtful girl with a heart of gold. Yet when it came to being popular with the other girls, she wasn't even on their radar.

Lizzy put on her favorite shorts and the t-shirt she had gotten just for school. As she stood in front of her bedroom mirror to critique her clothing and hair, she thought that it wasn't fair that she had curly, out-of-control hair when her friends had pretty, straight hair. Even her mom's hair was straight with golden brown highlights. Her mom had a natural beauty that ran much deeper than the surface. Lizzy didn't like her hazel eyes or the dimples in her cheeks. But she did love the navy blue shorts and blue and white striped t-shirt she had picked out for her first day. It was always exciting to get new clothes and school supplies for a brand new school year. She noticed the bruise on her right knee from Max tackling her for the doggie treat she was holding the other day. He really needs obedience school, thought Lizzy.

The sweet smell of cinnamon toast drifted into her bedroom. If she didn't hurry to the kitchen, Max would probably eat her toast as a snack! As she began running towards the kitchen, Max decided it would be fun to race. Lizzy slid in her socks into the kitchen at the same time as Max, but she was able to hop into her chair and push her plate back just before Max got his nose near her toast. He had recently figured out that he was now tall enough to steal food off the kitchen table!

"I won that time, Max!" laughed Lizzy. "You're just going to have to eat dog food today."

After breakfast, Lizzy's stomach had settled, and she was ready to face the day. Soon Lizzy and her mom were on their way to school. The weather in northern Ohio was still hot and humid. Lizzy was glad she could wear shorts for the first couple weeks of school before the onset of cooler weather. It was hard to think about the summer coming to an end, since it was her favorite time of year.

As they neared the school, Lizzy's stomach started doing flip flops. Mom could sense Lizzy's apprehension. "When I'm nervous," Mom said gently, "I try to remember that God's Word says that we should be anxious for nothing. Thinking of that helps me to relax a bit and just leave everything in God's hands. I will be praying for you today!"

"I know, Mom...thanks.......I'll be praying, too. Oh! I see Jordan! Bye, Mom!" Lizzy yelled as she slammed the car door and ran to meet Jordan. What would Lizzy do without Jordan! She was her very best friend. While their looks were quite different from each other, their personalities worked perfectly together. It seemed they knew just what the other was thinking without saying a word. Jordan was definitely the leader, while Lizzy bounced merrily along, happy to follow her lead. Jordan had long, straight brown hair, while Lizzy's was a lighter brown full of unruly curls. She was constantly battling the tangles because she wanted to wear her hair long, like most of the girls in her class. Jordan had beautiful dark brown eyes, unlike Lizzy's, but their height was the most prominent difference between the two. Jordan was tall like most of the other 6th grade girls at Riverside Middle School, while Lizzy was the shortest girl in her class.

Jordan was the type of girl who saw what she wanted and went after it. She was organized and determined. Although Jordan did have a few challenges due to her family dynamics, she hid her feelings about it very well.

As Lizzy and Jordan entered the school, they saw their friend, Jenna, and the three headed to their homeroom together. After a quick check-in, the girls made their way to their lockers. As Lizzy approached her locker, she heard that dreaded familiar voice.

"Hey Lizard. I see you still have that bird's nest on top of your head,"

Kaylee Brooks, a.k.a. 'Miss I've-got-it-all-and-I-know- it,' was definitely not Lizzy's favorite person!

"Why does she always pick on me?" groaned Lizzy under her breath as Kaylee was walking away. Why can't I ever think of something to say back to her? she thought. Instead, I act like I'm afraid of her. Jordan would know what to say. She always knows what to say to Kaylee and her cronies. Maybe that's why they leave her alone!

Oh no, thought Lizzy as she searched in her backpack. Where did I put my locker combination? I can't be late for math! After finally getting into her locker and grabbing her math notebook, Lizzy bolted to class.

"Well, hello Miss Thompson, it's nice to see you finally decided to join us. Maybe tomorrow you'll be a little more prompt," scolded Mr. Phillips.

Of all the teachers in school, Lizzy did NOT want to get on Mr. Phillip's bad side. He was very intelligent but difficult to please. He had an overpowering personality that compensated for his short, scrawny stature.

As Lizzy quickly slid into the last available seat in the room, the entire classroom filled with snickers. How embarrassing, thought Lizzy. Finally, Mr. Phillips was able to quiet everyone down and began teaching the math lesson for the day. Since it was only review from the previous year, Lizzy felt encouraged. At least I understand all of this so far, thought Lizzy. Maybe math will actually be easier this year!

After 20 minutes of simple equations, math class was nearly over. Things were looking up!

"Hey Lizard, got anything nesting in there yet?" taunted Kristin.

"Funny, Kristin," Jordan quietly shot back. "Did Kaylee pay you to say that? It's pretty original!"

Suddenly, Mr. Phillips glared at Jordan. "Jordan, do you have something you'd like to share with the class?" he asked.

"Uh…. no…..I'm good," said Jordan with a flushed face.

"Then, please pay attention," he reprimanded.

"Oh, I have a question, Mr. Phillips," said Kaylee as she quickly raised her hand. "Can we do extra credit in math this year? I really want to make sure I keep up my 4.0 GPA."

"Yes, I will be offering extra credit again this year," responded Mr. Phillips. I'm sure you'll have no problem keeping your grades up, Kaylee. Now that's the attitude I like to see! If everyone in this class took math more seriously, we'd have a more successful year of learning."

Wow, Kaylee sure knows how to manipulate Mr. Phillips, thought Lizzy. If he only knew what she was really like!

Suddenly the bell rang. "Saved by the bell," Jordan said under her breath. "We're off to gym class!"

CHAPTER 2

Volleyball... My Fave... LOL!

"Be strong and courageous..."

"Do you know what we're doing in gym today?" Lizzy questioned Jordan.

"I looked in the gym this morning and saw the volleyball net set up," replied Jordan. "I love volleyball!"

"I don't," groaned Lizzy. "Why is there a ball involved in every single sport? There's basketball, softball, volleyball, and even soccer. What about people who can't even catch a ball, like me? Why can't we ride bikes or do gymnastics? I can walk on my hands now! Hey, I know ...we could race while walking on our hands. We could call it... a hand relay! I'd be great at that!"

"Oh Lizzy, you're funny!" laughed Jordan as they headed into the locker room to change into their gym clothes. When all of the 6th graders had changed clothes and entered the gym, Mr. Keebler blew his shrill whistle to get everyone's attention.

"Alright ladies and gentlemen," he barked. "I understand that this is the first day of school, but your schedule states that gym class begins at 9:15 AM, not 9:17. From now on, anyone who is not dressed and ready to go at 9:15 sharp will run three laps for every minute they are late. Do I make myself clear?"

"Yes, Mr. Keebler," the class mumbled in unison.

"As you people can see," continued Mr. Keebler, "I have the volleyball net set up. Kaylee Brooks and....Jonathon Fisher, you will be team captains for our volleyball game today. We will be doing a schoolyard pick. You two can take turns choosing one person to be on your team until everyone is chosen. Jonathon, you may go first."

"Okay," answered Jonathon excitedly. "Um..... I choose..... Ben."

"Alright, Kaylee, it's your turn to choose," continued Mr. Keebler.

"Okay, I choose Kristin!" Kaylee yelled out.

Oh great, thought Lizzy. I'm going to be the last one chosen, like usual. The teams were quickly being filled as Lizzy waited anxiously for her name to be called. As each person was chosen, Lizzy felt a little more dread and embarrassment.

"And last but not least, Lizzy. It looks like you are on Kaylee's team," stated Mr. Keebler.

Last one chosen again, thought Lizzy. And to top it off, I'm on Kaylee's team. Ugh! Could life get any worse?

"Alright people," barked Mr. Keebler. "I'm assuming everyone remembers the rules of volleyball from last year. Kaylee, your team will have the first serve. Remember if you touch the net, it's the other team's point. If the ball touches the net going over, it's fair play. Each time a serve is made and the other team fails to return it, the serving team scores a point. The first team to hit 25 points wins. Remember you need to win by at least two points. Everyone got it?"

The class nodded their heads in agreement.

"Okay, Kaylee," continued Mr. Keebler, "go ahead and serve after my whistle. Stay on your toes people!"

The game began and Lizzy dreaded every minute of it! Each time the ball came near her, she would back away to let another team member run to her area and hit the ball. Whenever Lizzy's team scored, Kaylee and Kristin would yell, "Y-E-A Team!" and give each other a high five. Soon, the whole team was participating...everyone except Lizzy, who clearly didn't want to be there.

"Nice leadership, girls!" Mr. Keebler yelled to Kaylee and Kristin. "Lizzy, you need to return that ball and not run away from it."

"Ok," agreed Lizzy. "I'll really try to get the next one that comes to me."

It didn't take long before the ball came right to Lizzy. She crouched down, put her arms in front of her, and made contact with the ball. I actually hit it, thought Lizzy excitedly. It was a hard hit. It flew up, sailed backwards, and.............slammed right into Kaylee's face!

CHAPTER 3

Anyone Have an Ice Pack

"Love is patient, love is kind..."

"AAHHHHHH!" Kaylee sat down with her hands covering her face. "You did that on purpose, Lizard! I think my nose might be broken! Call 9-1-1 or something! I need help right NOW!"

Oh no, thought Lizzy, what have I done? "Sorry, Kaylee, are you alright?" asked Lizzy meekly.

"No!" yelled Kaylee. "Is my whole face black and blue? It hurts so bad! I probably have a concussion, too!"

"Wow! She's a poet and doesn't even know it," Ben yelled out, causing a few of the boys to laugh.

"Kristin, why don't you take Kaylee to the nurse's office," suggested Mr. Keebler. "See if you can get an ice pack for her face. You're going to be fine, Kaylee."

"Okay, Mr Keebler," responded Kristin. "Come on, Kaylee, let me help you get to the nurse's office. You poor thing! I can't believe that Lizard did that to you!

Kristin grabbed Kaylee's arm and led her out of the

gym. As Kaylee was staggering out, she looked at Lizzy sneakily and smiled, just before letting out another loud wail.

"Enough volleyball," Mr. Keebler called out. "Class is almost over. Run three laps, then hit the locker rooms!"

Oh no, thought Lizzy. Now the whole class will be mad at me. Everyone knows Mr. Keebler only makes us run laps when he's mad!

"Way to go, Lizard," yelled Jonathon. "We just love running laps. NOT!"

"Don't let him bother you, Lizzy," said Jenna, as she approached Lizzy. "It's not like you did it on purpose. Accidents happen."

"Yeah. Did you see all of the drama Kaylee caused just to get Mr. Keebler's sympathy?" asked Jordan as she and Jenna began running beside Lizzy. "She acted like she was going to die! Then when Mr. Keebler looked away, she smiled at Lizzy. What a drama queen! I bet she could win an Oscar for acting!"

"I know," said Jenna. "She just knows she can get to you, Lizzy. That's why she tries so hard. I'll bet if you acted like you didn't care, she wouldn't pick on you so much."

"But that's easier said than done," groaned Lizzy. "I do care about what people think of me. I hate it when they're mean to me... or mad at me!"

"Well, there's not much you can do about Kaylee," said Jordan. "She's just like that. I really don't know what her problem is."

Soon the students made their way to the locker rooms to change clothes. After a calm social studies class, it was time for lunch. Lizzy rushed into the cafeteria to claim a table before all the good seats were taken. She needed to save seats for her two best buddies, Jordan and Jenna.

It was fun having Jenna around. She had previously been friends with Kaylee, but after a falling out during the middle of fifth grade, she started hanging out with Lizzy and Jordan.

Jenna was cute and tall with green eyes and freckles on her nose. Her blonde hair was so long and shiny that many girls envied her. She had limitless energy and always had a smile on her face. Jenna was successful at EVERYTHING she attempted! Lizzy couldn't figure out if Jenna was successful because of her energy and optimism, or if she was optimistic because she was seemingly good at everything she did. She had no idea why Jenna would want to hang out with Jordan and her, but she was glad that she did. She definitely brought enthusiasm and a positive attitude to the trio.

CHAPTER 4

What's That Smell?

"Be kind to one another..."

As Lizzy entered the cafeteria, she heard the clanging sound of silverware and muffled laughter. The balminess in the air along with the comforting smell of food brought back pleasant memories of previous school years.

There was one table available with three empty seats together. Lizzy raced to the table to claim the seats. Unfortunately, they just happened to be at the same table as Kaylee, Kristin, and Becca. As Lizzy approached the table, all three girls plugged their noses.

"Ew, do you smell that?" moaned Kristin.

"I don't smell anything," said Lizzy naively.

"It smells like........a lizard!" said Kaylee. All three girls burst out in laughter at the same time. Even the boys at the end of the table were laughing.

As Lizzy held back the tears, Jordan and Jenna joined her at the table.

"What's so funny?" asked Jenna.

"Oh, nothing important," said Becca. "It's just an inside joke. You wouldn't understand it."

"Yeah," said Kaylee. "I guess Lizard doesn't appreciate our humor." Once again the girls began laughing.

"Hey, Lizzy," Jordan said trying to change the subject, "are you going to the football game Friday night? It should be an awesome game. Fairfield is our biggest rival."

"I'm not sure yet, I'll have to ask my mom. Are you two going?" questioned Lizzy.

"My mom said I can go, but only if you're going," responded Jordan.

"Same with my mom!" added Jenna.

"Okay, I'll text you guys tonight to let you know if I can go," Lizzy said hopefully.

"It looks like Kaylee's broken nose healed pretty fast," whispered Jordan.

"Yeah," replied Jenna. "She's quite the drama queen. But at least you don't have anything to worry about now, Lizzy. She's fine."

"I guess so," whispered Lizzy. "If I could just find a way to stop her from being so mean to me."

"Hey, maybe you could hit her in the head with a ball again. It could work!" said Jordan. The three girls started laughing. Lizzy loved having the support of her friends. They always had a way of making her feel better when she was discouraged.

Once lunch was over, the day seemed to go faster for Lizzy. Recess was fun since she was able to hang out on the playground with Jordan and Jenna. Kaylee and her cronies were playing basketball with the boys. Once again most of the girls in Lizzy's class were trying to be Kaylee's best friend. They were constantly saying and doing nice things for her so that she would include them in her group. She seemed to have a strange power over them. Lizzy could never understand how such a mean girl could be so popular.

CHAPTER 5

*Does Anyone Have a Pair
of Scissors?*

"Who shall separate us..."

After recess, Lizzy, Jordan, and Jenna immediately made a beeline for the science room. They were the first ones there. Mr. Adams hadn't even arrived yet. Lizzy saw a white lab coat hanging from a hook on the wall. She walked over to it, put her back against the wall, and slid her arms into the sleeves, while it was still hanging on the hook.

"Look, I'm Mr. Adams," laughed Lizzy as she stood on her tippy toes.

"Well hello there," Mr. Adams laughed as he entered the room. I see you're just hanging around."

Lizzy's face turned bright red as she smiled. "Umm...hi...Mr. Adams. We were just waiting for class to start."

Jordan and Jenna started laughing as he smiled.

"You might want to get out of that coat before anyone else shows up for class," he chuckled.

Lizzy quickly slipped her left arm out. But as she leaned forward to pull out her right arm, she realized that her hair was stuck on the coat hook. She let out a loud groan. "Oh no, my hair's stuck!" Lizzy panicked.

Just as Jordan ran over to help, the students began filing into the room. Some students looked at Lizzy and laughed, while others asked what had happened. Soon, nearly the whole class was laughing and wondering how she had gotten stuck! Mr. Adams quickly went to his desk to grab a pair of scissors, while instructing the students to take their seats and quiet down. Jordan took a quick snip of Lizzy's hair and finally, she was free! Lizzy slinked quietly to her seat, wishing she could just disappear for the rest of the day.

Mr. Adams welcomed everyone and began to go over his list of rules and expectations for his students.

"I'm excited about science class this year," Mr. Adams began. "Since I already know most of you from last year, it should make your transition to 6th grade easier. We will be doing some fun projects and experiments this year. I hope to have everyone actively participate and enjoy this class. I expect all of you to treat one another with courtesy and respect. And, as in life, you will get out of this class what you put into it. If you all put forth 100% effort, I'm sure we'll have a very successful year."

Lizzy smiled at Jordan as if to say 'this will be a great class!' Jordan gave a quick thumbs up in agreement. When the bell rang, Mr. Adams called Lizzy to his desk.

"I hope you weren't too embarrassed by that little incident, Lizzy. I suggest you don't try on any more lab coats, at least not while they're still hanging up!" laughed Mr. Adams.

"No, I won't do that again!" Lizzy stated emphatically.

"Good idea! You'd better hurry to your next class. I'll see you tomorrow," instructed her teacher.

"Okay, thanks Mr. Adams!" said Lizzy as she left his classroom and quickly walked down the hallway to language arts.

Language arts and computer class flew by for Lizzy.

She was thankful there were no more run-ins with Kaylee and her cronies. The school day was finally over!

"Hey Lizzy, don't forget to text Jenna and me about the game," said Jordan as she walked by Lizzy's locker.

"Sure thing, I'll let you know as soon as I can. Bye," said Lizzy as she hurried outside to her mom's car.

"See you tomorrow!" said Jordan as she quickly walked to the bus line.

CHAPTER 6

Mmmm...Meatloaf!

"Bear one another's burdens..."

"Hi Mom," Lizzy said as she climbed into the car, feeling the cool relief from the car's air conditioner. She leaned forward and adjusted the vent, so the air would blow directly into her face.

"Ahhhh," Lizzy said before she leaned back and buckled her seat belt.

"Hi Honey," replied Mom. "How was your first day?"

"It was alright," Lizzy mumbled. "Oh, Jordan and Jenna want to know if I can go to the game Friday night. We're playing Fairfield!"

"Well, as a matter of fact," said Mom, while pulling the car into the street, "Dad and I were thinking about going and letting you bring a friend or two. Maybe we could pick them up on our way. You girls can sit in the student section, while we sit with the other parents."

"That sounds great, Mom!" Lizzy said excitedly. "I'll text them and let them know as soon as we get home!"

"Alright," replied Mom, "I'll call their parents and work out the details."

"Awesome! I can't wait until Friday!" added Lizzy.

"By the way," asked Mom, "how's Jordan doing?"

"She's good. Same old Jordo," answered Lizzy as she put her face directly in front of the cool air again.

"Did she have a nice time at her dad's?" Mom questioned.

"I don't know," answered Lizzy. "She said she'd rather spend summers at her mom's. Her dad's girlfriend moved in and they argue a lot, even in front of Jordan. I guess it was kind of weird for her."

"I'm sorry to hear that, Honey," replied Mom. "Maybe we should include them in our prayers."

"That's a good idea," said Lizzy. "So... what's for supper, I'm starving!"

"I'm making your favorite...meatloaf."

"Oh yummy!" squealed Lizzy while smiling. "We haven't had that in a long time."

"I thought you'd like a special meal to celebrate your first day back at school," replied Mom. "Did you have any problems finding your classrooms today?"

"No, but I couldn't remember my locker combination," groaned Lizzy. "Then I couldn't find the paper it's written on. When I finally got it open, I was late for math class."

"Did you get into trouble?" asked Mom quietly.

"Not really," replied Lizzy. "Mr. Phillips just said I need to work at being on time."

"You might want to get that combination memorized today," commented Mom. "Then you won't be late again."

"I know.... I think I have it memorized now," replied

Lizzy. "15 right two times ……. 18 left two times…….3 right one time …….or is it 6? No, it's 3."

"Why don't you think of it this way," suggested Mom "At age fifteen, you can get your driver's permit,…. at eighteen, you legally become an adult."

"I know!" said Lizzy. "I started preschool when I was three!"

"That's right," said Mom. "Now if you ever forget it, just think of those three things."

"Fifteen, eighteen, three. Got it! Thanks Mom," Lizzy said as they pulled into the driveway.

"Sure," replied Mom. "Maybe that will help your day go a little smoother."

"For sure!" Lizzy added. Mom unlocked the back door and let Lizzy enter the house first.

"I'm going to go text Jordan and Jenna about the game," Lizzy said as she grabbed a granola bar from the kitchen and began heading to her room.

Out of nowhere, her dog, Max, raced toward Lizzy and grabbed the granola bar from her hand.

"Give that back, Max!" scolded Lizzy. As Lizzy was chasing Max down the hallway, she called for Mom to help. "He's got my granola bar!"

Mom quickly joined in the chase. Soon, they were able to corner Max, and Lizzy slowly pried it out of his mouth.

"Good thing I hadn't unwrapped it yet!" exclaimed Lizzy. "Did you call Golden Paws today?"

"He's scheduled for a meet and greet on Friday," answered Mom in relief. "If they accept him into their class, he'll have his first session on Monday."

"Awesome! He really needs it!" exclaimed Lizzy as she walked to her room to text her friends about the football game.

"Make sure you get your homework done in time to set the table before dinner. We're eating at 6:00," replied Mom.

"Got it, Mom. And, no homework on my first day. Yay!" Lizzy said as she quickly shut her bedroom door to keep

Max out. As Lizzy entered her room she began texting best friends, Jordan and Jenna.

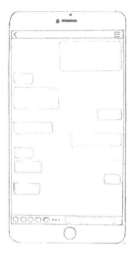

Liz: game's on. mom n dad r going. will pick u up on way. mom will call parents

Jen: yea!

Jor: can't wait! what r u wearing to sch. tom.?

Liz: idk y?

Jor: dress up?

Liz: as in a dress?

Jor: yep

Jen: cool

Liz: maybe

Jor: ttyl

Jen: c ya

With that, the girls were finished texting. After listening to her favorite playlist and winning a couple games on her phone, Lizzy looked through her bookbag, took out her math paper, and headed to the kitchen.

"Here's my math paper. A+!" Lizzy beamed.

"Great job, I'm proud of you!" said Mom.

Suddenly Max began barking and pacing the kitchen floor. "Max, quiet down!" commanded Lizzy. Just then, Dad walked into the kitchen.

"Hi, Honey," he said as he approached Mom and quickly kissed her. "Whoa, down boy!" laughed Dad as Max jumped up onto him and placed his front paws on his chest.

"How was your day?" he asked Mom. "Did you have any luck with Golden Paws?"

"We have a meet and greet Friday. If he's accepted, he'll start his obedience training next week," answered Mom.

"That's great news!" replied Dad. "IF... they accept him!" he laughed. "Hey Lizzy, how was school today?" asked Dad enthusiastically.

"It was alright," Lizzy replied.

"I'll bet it was nice to see everyone again, huh?" Dad asked.

"Yeah, it was fun seeing Jordan and Jenna."

"Did Jordan have a nice time over the summer with her dad?" he questioned.

"It was okay, I guess," Lizzy replied. "She told me that she would rather have stayed at her mom's though."

"Well, sometimes things can get a little complicated when there's a divorce," explained Dad. "I'm sure it's not easy for Jordan sharing a home with someone that she barely knows."

"Oh, you know about his girlfriend then?" asked Mom.

"Yes, Dad explained. "I ran into Jordan's dad at the hardware store a few weeks ago. He told me that his girlfriend had moved in last June. But when I asked him how Jordan felt about the living situation, he said he didn't know. Apparently he hadn't talked to her about it beforehand. It was an awkward moment to say the least. I feel bad for Jordan."

"I'm sure that isn't easy for her," replied Mom.

"I know," agreed Dad. "I wish parents would be more aware of how their decisions affect their children's lives... We'll have to keep Jordan in our prayers. All you can do, Lizzy, is to be the best friend you can be to her. She could really use a great friend right now! So... what are we having for dinner? It smells wonderful."

"Meatloaf!" said Lizzy.

"That sounds great. It's your favorite, huh Lizzy?" asked Dad.

"Yep," answered Lizzy. "I can't wait to eat, I'm starving! As long as Max doesn't get to it first!"

CHAPTER 7

Pray for HER? Are You Serious?!

"For all things work together for good..."

During dinner, Lizzy seemed a little more quiet than usual.

"Are you sure your day went alright?" asked Dad. "You seem awfully quiet."

"Did Kaylee call you names again?" asked Mom.

"Yeah, but that didn't bother me so much," answered Lizzy. "When I sat down for lunch, I had to sit at the same table with Kaylee, Kristin, Emma AND Becca. They all plugged their noses when I sat down. Then they said something smelled like a lizard! Everyone was laughing, even the boys! It was so embarrassing!"

"Hmm.... so what did you do?" asked Mom.

"I didn't do anything," Lizzy explained. "Jordan and Jenna got there right after that, so I just talked to them."

"It sounds like you dealt with it in a very mature way. I hope as the school year progresses, they'll be nicer to you," Mom said sympathetically.

"Well," replied Lizzy, "Kaylee's probably just mad because of gym class."

"Really? What happened in gym?" asked Dad.

"Well...," answered Lizzy, "we were playing   volleyball and when I returned the ball, it hit Kaylee right in the face! SMACK!"

"Oh no!" said Mom. "Was she alright?"

"Yeah, she had to go to the nurse's office to get an ice pack," replied Lizzy, "but she was okay. She was just really mad! She said that I did it on purpose, but I didn't!"

"Well, I'm glad she was all right," responded Mom. "Accidents do happen, especially in sports."

"I'm sorry you had to go through that, Kiddo,"   said Dad. "I know it can be rough at school sometimes. If the teasing ever gets too bad, I want you to promise to let your mom or me know. We would be happy to talk to the teachers or principal, if necessary. You know that we always have your back!"

"Okay Dad..... but please don't say anything to the teachers," Lizzy begged. "I have to see Kaylee everyday at school. If she knew I complained about her, she'd treat me even worse!"

"That's not how it works, Honey," answered Dad. "This would be in the strictest of confidence. The teachers would just have a heads up, so they could keep a better eye on how you're being treated by your classmates."

"Kaylee's really good at hiding it from the teachers!" exclaimed Lizzy. "And no matter how mean she is, everyone wants to be her best friend. Everyone, that is, except Jordan and Jenna. I just don't get it!"

"Not everything makes sense in life, nor is it always fair," said Dad. "But we need to hold our heads up and do the best we can. And pray a lot. In fact, maybe we should pray for Kaylee."

"Pray for her?! Why would we pray for someone who's so mean?" Lizzy asked bewildered.

"Because that's what God wants us to do," said Mom. "Remember the verse we learned last week in church? Matt. 5:44. 'Love your enemies and pray for those who persecute you.'"

"Yes.... I remember," mumbled Lizzy.

"Do you think Kaylee would fit into that category?" Dad questioned.

"I guess so." Lizzy said hesitantly. "But do you really think God would actually change her heart so that she would treat me better?"

"I don't have the answer to that, Honey," said Dad. "But prayer not only helps us communicate our feelings and our needs to the Lord, but it also helps to grow our faith. Only the Lord can change Kaylee's heart, but you could show her Godly love by the way you respond to her antics. Maybe someday she'll see what a beautiful person you are and want to be more like you."

"Okay," conceded Lizzy, "I'll give it a try and pray for her."

After dinner, Lizzy helped with the dishes and watched her favorite TV show. Soon it was time for a shower and bed. Before turning out the lights, Lizzy prayed:

"Dear Lord, it was kind of a rough day today. I hate being picked on! Please help Kaylee to treat me better. I don't know why she hates me so much but help me to forgive her. I want your light to shine through me. And also, give me a good day at school tomorrow......and..... help Jordan with her dad. Oh, and thanks for meatloaf...Amen."

Eph. 4:31 Be kind to one another, tenderhearted, forgiving one another as God in Christ forgave you.

CHAPTER 8

A BMW and a Horse?

"A cheerful heart is good for the soul..."

Afonter a good night's sleep, Lizzy awoke with a new sense of peace and hope. She was ready to take on a new day with a positive attitude and a determination to never let Kaylee Brooks bother her again.

As Mom was driving her to school, Lizzy sent up a silent prayer...

"Dear Lord, please help me to have a good day, and let Kaylee not pick on me today. Amen."

When Lizzy hopped out of the car in the school parking lot, she noticed Kaylee getting out of her sister's convertible. Kaylee slammed the door while yelling at her sister, Megan, to stay out of her business. She and Megan both looked angry. When Kaylee noticed Lizzy staring at her, she quickly looked away and immediately made a beeline for the front doors. She was definitely upset!

"Hi Lizzy," Jordan greeted her cheerily as Lizzy was approaching her locker.

"Hi Jordo," replied Lizzy.

"Hey Jordan, hey Lizzy," said Ben.

"What are you doing down here, Ben?" asked Jordan. "I thought your locker was down at the other end of the hall."

"It is," replied Ben, "but I saw Kaylee drive up and came down here to get a better look! Did you see that car? Sweet!"

"I saw it," mumbled Lizzy.

"It's a Beemer!" exclaimed Ben. "Looks brand new! Wish my parents had a car like that!"

"Hi guys, what's up?" Jenna joined in.

"Hey Jenna. Ben was just drooling over the Beemer that Kaylee's sister drives," Lizzy complained.

"Beemer?" Jenna asked.

"Yeah, you know, a BMW, convertible, brand new!" said Ben.

"Wow, I bet that wasn't cheap!" exclaimed Jenna.

"For sure! Nothing Kaylee has is cheap!" replied Ben. "Hey," said Ben jokingly, "What's the difference between a horse and a BMW?"

"A horse... and a BMW?" repeated Lizzy with a puzzled look on her face.

"Give up?" asked Ben anxiously.

"Okay.... I give," said Jenna.

"Me too," said Lizzy and Jordan in unison. "What IS the difference between a horse and a BMW, Ben?" asked Jordan.

"A BMW has more horsepower. Get it, more HORSE power."

"We get it," said Jenna smiling.

"Why isn't anyone laughing? That was funny!" accused

Ben.

"That was kind of funny, Ben," said Lizzy.

"Yeah, but maybe when you graduate, you might want to rethink your idea of becoming a comedian," laughed Jordan.

"Ouch!" replied Ben. "I have some real critics here! A comedian is never appreciated in his hometown."

"Just kidding, Ben!" replied Jordan. "You know we're your biggest fans! Whoa, we have three minutes to get to homeroom. We better get moving."

Jordan led the way to homeroom and the four slid into their seats just before the bell rang.

"Alright class, I need all eyes and ears focused on me," instructed Mrs. Wagner. "As you know, our open house will be two weeks from Thursday at 7:00 p.m. Please raise your hand if your family is planning to   attend." As the students raised their hands, Mrs. Wagner continued."

"Good, it looks like most of you will be here; that's wonderful! Also, remember that your field trip   permission slips are due by next Monday. Any questions?" Mrs. Wagner asked and waited for a response. "Okay, since there are no hands raised , I will take that as a no. Alright then, have a great day!"

Just then the bell rang and the students exited their homerooms and headed out to their first period classes.

CHAPTER 9

Sing

"Take heed lest you fall......"

"**H**ey Lizzy, I really like your book bag," Jenna said as she, Lizzy, and Jordan were walking to math class together.

"Thanks," Lizzy responded.

"Where did you get it?" asked Jenna.

"My mom got it at a garage sale. It was never used! Can you believe that the tags were still on it and it only cost $2.00?" Lizzy asked proudly.

"A garage sale!" Kaylee announced loudly as she trailed behind them, eavesdropping on their conversation. "Who goes to garage sales? Oh my gosh!" Kaylee rolled her eyes and sighed.

"Well, my mom does," defended Lizzy. "And she finds some really great deals!"

Kaylee stood speechless for a moment at Lizzy's response while Lizzy, Jenna, and Jordan continued walking to class.

"Wow, Lizzy," said Jordan. "I think that's the first time

you've ever stood up to Kaylee. Well done!"

"Yeah, I guess so, and hopefully I won't ever have to do that again!" Lizzy sighed. "If I knew Kaylee was walking behind us, I wouldn't have told you where I got it," moaned Lizzy.

"Try not to let her bother you, Lizzy," replied Jordan. "Remember, she just likes to pick on people."

"Especially ME!" Lizzy groaned.

After another easy math class, it was time for choir. Choir was much more enjoyable for Lizzy than gym class. If you weren't a good singer, you could sing softly so no one would know how bad your voice really was. The boys were great at singing softly! But not Kaylee and Kristin. They had beautiful voices and made sure everyone knew it!

As Lizzy entered the choir room, she saw a very short woman with curly brown hair that had more frizz than curls. She was wearing a bright red floral shirt with orange and brown checkered pants. Her glasses looked too big for her small face and she wore green tennis shoes to top it off. Lizzy wondered if she dressed in the dark at home. That could be the only reasonable explanation for her outrageous attire, unless she was color blind!

There were a few snickers and whispers from the girls in Lizzy's class, and even from some of the boys. Lizzy was hopeful that the students would treat her with respect.

"Okay, boys and girls, please quiet down,"   instructed the melodic voice. "My name is Mrs. Hobner and I'm the new choir director. I hope all of you had a wonderful summer and are ready to get focused on singing. La...La...La... I'm going to be passing out music for you to practice today. Since we have an open house coming up, I would like to open it with a couple of songs from the choir. That way your parents can hear your beautiful voices. We will practice on the risers that are on the stage, so you will be comfortable singing there for the open house. I'm sure that all of you remember your vocal groups from last year. Let's have the bass singers in the back row, in front of the bass we will have the tenors, the next row will be the altos, with sopranos in the front row. Students, if you're ready, you may proceed to the risers."

As the students filed onto the stage and to the risers, the girls started pushing their way towards Kaylee. Three girls wanted to stand next to her and it became a bit of a shoving match. Lizzy was on the end in the front row watching the scuffle as Mrs. Hobner was sorting through her music. Suddenly, one girl shoved another in the row directly behind Lizzy. She lunged forward into Lizzy, which sent Lizzy flying straight off the edge of the risers! As she attempted to stand up, her left foot went over the edge of the stage. Lizzy fell off the stage and hit the floor with a loud thud!

CHAPTER 10

Take a Bow!

"Sing to the Lord a new song...."

Suddenly Mrs. Hobner's head shot up at the noise. "Oh my goodness. What happened? Are you alright?" asked Mrs. Hobner.

"Um... I'm okay," said Lizzy quietly. "I guess I just kind of lost my balance."

"Well, you're going to have to be more careful!" Mrs. Hobner instructed. "We can't have that happening during our performance. Goodness me, your parents would think...well...I don't know what they'd think, but it wouldn't be good!"

Lizzy climbed back onto the risers trying to hide her embarrassment.

"Are you alright?" whispered Jordan.

"I'm fine," mumbled Lizzy.

"Why didn't you just tell her what happened?" questioned Jordan.

"And have everyone mad at me? Forget it. Anyways, it was just an accident," answered Lizzy.

"You have to stop letting those girls push you around , Lizzy, literally!" exclaimed Jordan.

"If something bad happens, then I'll say something, okay?" Lizzy replied.

"Okay, deal," Jordan conceded.

"Now where did I put my tuner?" Mrs. Hobner questioned. "Oh dear, I had it just a minute ago."

"Is that your tuner on the podium, Mrs. Hobner?" asked Kaylee in her sweetest voice.

"Oh, you are such a dear. I think I'd lose my head if it wasn't attached!" laughed Mrs.Hobner.

"Well, that would be kind of creepy," said Ben. "Walking around without a head! Wow, you'd never get A-HEAD in life. You could never be A HEAD of a big corporation!"

As the class started laughing, Ben took a bow.

"Alright, we need to get down to business," laughed Mrs. Hobner. "Otherwise, we'll never get A-HEAD of schedule! Oh dear, I just made a funny! Okay, class…let's start singing the scales to get our voices warmed up."

Choir went by pretty quickly after Lizzy's embarrassing moment. Everyone seemed pleased with Mrs. Hobner's choice of songs. She wasn't the most organized person, but she seemed like a great choir teacher.

Just before the bell rang, Mrs. Hobner instructed, "Please practice these songs at home, that is if you can remember them. Pass your music sheets to the left so I can collect them. Students on the ends, please bring me the music sheets. Thank you and have a marvelous, musical day!!"

CHAPTER 11

Did You Say Something?

"Perhaps they will listen…"

"**O**nto social studies," replied Jenna. "Hey, are you alright, Lizzy?"

"I'm okay, just a little embarrassed," Lizzy answered.

"That was quite a fall you took! Mrs. Hobner didn't even see what happened," Jordan sympathized.

"I know," said Lizzy. "She was too busy trying to find her music. I sure like the songs she picked for the open house though."

"Me too!" exclaimed Jenna.

As the girls entered social studies class, Kaylee glared at Lizzy. Lizzy quickly looked away, hoping that if she just ignored her, maybe Kaylee would leave her alone.

"Alright class, listen up," barked Mr. Elling. "We have a lot of material to cover. The harder you work in class today, the greater your chance for no homework."

Soon they were reading aloud the social studies lesson. Lizzy tried to pay attention, but every time she looked up, Kaylee was glaring at her.

"Who wants to read aloud the next paragraph?" asked Mr. Elling. No one in the classroom raised a hand to volunteer to read, so Mr. Elling looked directly at Lizzy.

"Lizzy?" he asked"

"Huh?" Lizzy responded in a surprised voice, wondering which paragraph they were on.

"Would you please read aloud the next paragraph?" Mr. Elling asked.

"Umm...," hesitated Lizzy.

"Weren't you following along?" asked Mr. Elling in a frustrated tone. "Kaylee, can you please read the next paragraph?"

"Sure thing, Mr. Elling," Kaylee said, while smirking at Lizzy.

As Kaylee read, Lizzy silently scolded herself for not having paid attention. Lizzy was embarrassed once again and the class seemed to drag on endlessly. After the bell rang, Kaylee shot Lizzy a very smug look as she walked past Lizzy's desk.

"Well, maybe my prayer won't be answered today," thought Lizzy. " But hopefully someday it will be, and Kaylee will actually be a nicer person."

"Hey, Lizzy, don't forget to save us a seat in the cafeteria," Jordan said as the girls exited the classroom. Lizzy hurried to her locker to get her lunchbox.

"I'm on it. See you there!" Lizzy answered.

CHAPTER 12

Have a Cookie

"Go, eat your food with gladness..."

T oday I'm going to get a table before Kaylee and her
cronies get here, thought Lizzy as she raced into the
cafeteria. That way we can sit far away from them.

A few of the sixth grade boys were sitting at a table as
Lizzy walked by. "Hey Lizard," called out Brent. "We were
thinking about taking up a collection for you." "Why?"
asked Lizzy hesitantly.

"So we can buy you a new bookbag!" Brent said mock-
ing her.

All the boys at the table started laughing. Just then
Jonathon gave Brent a high five.

"Good one, Brent!" said Jonathon.

"Well, I happen to LIKE my bookbag!" Lizzy exclaimed
as she walked to a table on the other side of the room. After
claiming an empty table, she started unpacking her lunch.
To her surprise, a note from her mom fell out of her lunchbox.

'Have a great day Lizzy. I'm praying for you!'

Love, Mom

Suddenly, Lizzy felt a sense of peace. She knew that whatever each day brought, her parents would be praying for her and supporting her. That always lightened her mood.   Soon Jordan and Jenna joined Lizzy at the table. Lizzy happened to notice Kaylee and her friends a few tables away. As she took a bite of her sandwich, she noticed that Kaylee, Kristin, and Becca were looking at her and laughing.

They're probably laughing about my bookbag thought Lizzy. Ughh! I'm just going to ignore them.

After another glance at the girls, Lizzy noticed that Kaylee was once again glaring at her.

Dear Lord, Lizzy silently prayed as she looked down at her table, please help me to not let those mean girls bother me.

"So, Lizzy...what do you think?" asked Jenna.

"What?" replied Lizzy.

"I don't think you heard a word we said," accused Jordan.

"Oh, sorry. I was just thinking about something else," Lizzy admitted.

"What's so important that you can't listen to us?" asked Jordan defensively.

"It's nothing, really," said Lizzy.

"Well," said Jenna, "like I was saying... my mom said that if it's alright with your parents, we can all spend the night at my house after the game Friday night. So...what do you think?"

"Sounds great!" exclaimed Lizzy. "I'll check with Mom when I get home and text you. She'll probably let me stay over."

"Hey, we'll have to plan something fun to do Saturday morning," said Jenna.

"I know!" said Jordan. "We can play volleyball!"

"Very funny!" Lizzy laughed.

"Speaking of funny," said Jenna, "guess where I got MY book bag, Lizzy?"

"Where?" Lizzy questioned. "At the Goodwill store," she whispered. All three girls started laughing.

"Sorry I didn't back you up with Kaylee about the book bag. She just caught me off guard. I didn't know what to say!" explained Jenna.

"Oh, that's okay, you don't want to be on Kaylee's bad side anyways," lamented Lizzy. "So...I guess that can be our little secret. Now if you ever upset me, I can always tell Kaylee about YOUR bookbag!" Lizzy laughed.

"Okay, you got me," giggled Jenna. "I promise I'll never make you mad!" All three girls started laughing.

"Hey, are you going to eat that cookie?" asked Lizzy.

"Nope, you can have it Lizzy, I'm stuffed!" moaned Jordan. "I honestly don't understand how you can eat so much and stay so skinny, Lizzy!"

"Well, I may not be good at volleyball, but at least I'm good at eating!" laughed Lizzy.

CHAPTER 13

I Need My Shades to Calm the Glare!

'For where you have envy...'

"Hey Lizzy, has Kaylee been glaring at you this whole lunch period?" asked Jenna.

"Yes!" exclaimed Lizzy. "I think she was really surprised when I stood up for myself about my book bag. My response must have made her mad."

"Oh, don't let her bother you," added Jenna. "She's been like that for years. Anyways, she's probably just jealous of you."

"Jealous?" Lizzy questioned. "Now you sound like Ben, a real comedian!"

"Well," said Jenna. "She may be rich... popular... smart..."

"And pretty!" exclaimed Lizzy.

"Yes," continued Jenna. "But, I don't think she has a very good family life."

"What do you mean?" asked Lizzy.

"Well....did you hear her share with the homeroom teacher that her parents won't be attending the open house?" asked Jenna

"Yes...," both girls replied

"And...have you noticed that her parents are never at any of her events?" continued Jenna.

"Now that you mention it, I guess so," Lizzy answered.

"Well...I've been to her house a lot of times before," continued Jenna, "and I don't even know what her parents look like. They're always working or traveling. I've never even seen them before!"

"Really?" asked Lizzy incredulously.

"No way!" exclaimed Jordan.

"Yes way!" continued Jenna. "Her sister, Megan, drops her off at her school events, but she never stays to watch her. She acts like HER life is too important to be bothered with Kaylee's. Sometimes Kaylee's nanny drops her off at her school activities, too."

"But, it still doesn't make sense," replied Lizzy. "Why in the world would she be jealous of ME?"

"Well," answered Jenna, "your mom always helps out at school, she's on the P.T.A....she even goes on all the field trips with our class. Kaylee's probably jealous of that."

"I don't see how that could cause anyone to be jealous," commented Lizzy.

"I don't know," replied Jordan. "It could be true. You do have great parents, Lizzy."

"That's true," continued Lizzy. "But our house is old and small, and I don't even wear new clothes all the time, like Kaylee does."

"Material things aren't always as important to people as you think they are, Lizzy," added Jenna. "I'd rather have great parents who care about me than lots of stuff anyday!"

"So…," interrupted Jordan, "you've been in her house before? What's it like? Spill it!"

"It's huge!" exclaimed Jenna. "It's got four bathrooms, six bedrooms and an indoor pool!"

"No way!" said Jordan.

"It's an awesome house," replied Jenna.

"No wonder she does so well on the swim team," stated Jordan.

"She has trophies and ribbons all over her room," continued Jenna.

"Wow, that must be nice," mumbled Lizzy.

"For sure!" said Jordan. "Hey, we better quit talking so much and start eating! The bell is going to ring soon and we don't want to be late for science class."

"Okay, let's hurry 'n eat!" Lizzy mumbled with her mouth full.

CHAPTER 14

Inventions 101

"...the bird was first, ready to lay eggs"

Soon the girls filed into the science room. As everyone took their seats, Mr. Adams looked at the students and smiled.

"Good afternoon, ladies and gentlemen. Over the next week, we're going to be learning about inventions and how they have influenced our modern world today. Your homework assignment for this week will be to write a short paper about what you believe is THE most important invention to date. This needs to be something that has completely changed our world. I'd like you to put a good amount of thought into this and you may even get your parents' input. There is no right or wrong answer, as long as you support your reasons with detailed facts to support your opinion. Your papers are to be typed and turned in to me on Friday. After I have collected all of the reports, we'll list your inventions on the board. I will get your reports graded and pass them back to you on Monday. After we've debated them thoroughly, we'll vote on what you believe is the most important, life changing invention. Whew! I know that was a lot of instructions! Do you have any questions?" Kaylee's hand immediately shot up. "Yes, Kaylee?" asked Mr. Adams.

"Can it be ANYTHING at all? Even the Smartphone?"

"Sure," he replied, "provided it has impacted our world in a major way. Great question, Kaylee. Any other questions? Alright, moving on. I'd like you to take your Science books and turn to Chapter 2 beginning on page 13...."

As class continued, Lizzy's mind was wandering to every invention she could think of. She would definitely have to bounce some ideas off her parents tonight. After a few minutes, the bell rang.

"Language arts is next," said Jordan, matter of factly.

"That's my favorite class, next to recess," said Lizzy excitedly.

"And I thought your favorite class was gym!" teased Jordan.

"Very funny, Jordo!" laughed Lizzy.

"So, Lizzy," said Ben as they entered language arts class, "if a rooster sits on the peak of barn roof facing north and lays an egg, will the egg roll down the east side or west side of the barn roof?"

"Um......I don't know, the east side?" asked Lizzy hesitantly.

"Nope," crooned Ben. "Seriously? Roosters don't lay eggs!"

"Okay, you got me again!" laughed Lizzy.

CHAPTER 15

Write Away!

*"I have written these things that
you may know..."*

As everyone began to take their seats, Mrs. Weichers greeted her students.

"Good afternoon. I hope you had a great day yesterday and are getting back into the routine of school. As I mentioned yesterday, we will be doing many types of writing this year, which will include keeping a journal. Oh..., I thought I heard some groaning from the boys. If you all keep an open mind, you may discover that you enjoy writing. Okay, to begin with, please raise your hand if you have ever tried a food that you thought you wouldn't like, but actually enjoyed. ...Jonathon, what was it that you tried?"

"Baked sweet potatoes," replied Jonathon. "My mom made me try one, and surprisingly enough, it was good, but I did put a lot of cinnamon and sugar on it!"

"That's great," continued Mrs. Weichers. "Anyone else? Yes, Lizzy?"

"I tried crab legs at a fancy restaurant this summer. When I cracked open the leg, the juice squirted out and hit my dad right in the eye! But I really liked the taste!" laughed Lizzy.

"That's funny, Lizzy," replied Mrs. Weichers. "Okay, has anyone ever tried a new activity that you didn't want to do, but found that you enjoyed it?....Jenna?"

"My dad took me fishing last summer," replied Jenna. "I didn't think I'd like it, but it was fun! Especially since I caught more fish than he did!"

"That's great, Jenna!" her teacher encouraged. "Anyone else? Yes, Ben?"

"This summer, my granny taught me how to knit. It was really fun, but hard!" replied Ben. "I even made a scarf for myself, but it came out a little crooked and way too long."

"You should really knit a purse to match your scarf," laughed Kaylee. "You'd look so pretty!"

The class erupted in laughter and Mrs. Weichers quickly reprimanded those involved. "That was totally uncalled for, Kaylee." She continued, "As you can see, we don't always know if we'll enjoy something until we try it. You may be surprised at how much fun you will have keeping a journal this year! Please save your judgment until after trying it, okay?"

The boys weren't buying it, but most of the girls were interested in the idea, especially Lizzy. She couldn't wait to get started writing in her new notebook!

When language arts concluded, Lizzy assured her friends that she would hurry to computer class to save them a seat. Since there was no assigned seating, Lizzy wanted first choice. She was hoping to sit in the back row, since her keyboarding skills weren't the best. Lizzy was afraid that by sitting in one of the front rows, her inexperience in keyboarding would be exposed. She certainly didn't want to be the brunt of ANOTHER joke.

As Lizzy neared her computer classroom, she overheard Kaylee bragging to Kristin. "Everything I'm wearing today is new, even my socks. I'm going shopping after school today so I can get another bookbag. I need to switch my bookbags up for school. It gets so tiring using the same old boring one every day."

"Wow," lamented Kristin, "My mom only lets me get one bookbag a year."

"I can have as many as I want," continued Kaylee. "I have to keep up with the new styles, you know."

Lizzy secretly rolled her eyes as she walked past Kaylee and Kristin. 'Oh Dear Lord, she prayed, please help me to be kind. It's so hard to be nice to someone like her!'

CHAPTER 16

Just the Right Type

*"Do you see someone skilled
in their work?..."*

As Lizzy entered the computer room, she was happy to find three empty seats in the back row. Kaylee and Kristin sat in the front row, as usual. The first two rows filled up quickly as Kaylee's classmates were battling for the seats nearest to her. Mrs. Garcia instructed the students to access Monkey Tail Typing on their personal laptops and complete Lessons 4-6.

After twenty minutes of practice, Lizzy discovered that the more she typed, the quicker and more accurate she became. She was beginning to feel more confident about her typing skills, until Kaylee raised her hand.

"Yes, Kaylee?" asked Mrs. Garcia.

"What do we do when we've finished the lessons?" asked Kaylee.

"You may want to repeat the lessons to work on your speed and accuracy," instructed Mrs. Garcia.

"But I just whizzed through all of the assigned lessons

and I scored a 99% on my accuracy," bragged Kaylee.

"Then, just wait patiently until the rest of the class finishes," replied her teacher.

"Okay, Mrs. Garcia," Kaylee replied sweetly. Kaylee began to drum her fingers on her desk and let out an occasional sigh, while waiting for everyone to finish. Soon, she took a bottle of cherry scented lip gloss out of her purse. After smelling it and sighing, she rolled it on her lips.

Lizzy was desperately trying to concentrate on her assignment, but the strong fruity scent distracted Lizzy from her work. I wonder if Mom's going to buy popsicles today. I just love popsicles! Every time she heard the drumming sound, she became more and more annoyed.

"Ugh!" Lizzy blurted out emphatically.

"Are you having problems with your computer?" Mrs. Garcia asked Lizzy with concern.

"No, I'm fine," Lizzy answered meekly.

"Well, if you have any questions, feel free to ask me. That's why I'm here," replied Mrs. Garcia.

"Okay, I will," Lizzy quietly answered. She finished up her lessons just before the bell rang.

I need to work on my typing speed, thought Lizzy. I don't like being one of the last ones to finish. It's too embarrassing, especially with Kaylee and her friends watching!

"Please straighten up your work space and push your chairs in. Have a good evening," Mrs. Garcia instructed as the bell rang. "And...if you are able to practice your typing skills at home, please do so."

Soon the students made their way to their lockers to pack up their bookbags for the day. Kaylee and three of her friends slowly walked past Lizzy's locker. They all gave Lizzy a fake smile and then immediately burst out in laughter.

Perfect ending to a perfect day, Lizzy thought sarcastically. Dear Lord, please help me to be strong and not get discouraged, Lizzy silently prayed.

As Lizzy was finishing up at her locker, Ben walked up behind her.

"Two down, 178 to go," stated Ben.

"What?" asked Lizzy.

"We just finished two days of school, so now we have 178 days left in sixth grade," replied Ben matter-of-factly.

"Oh great," responded Lizzy. "That's not very encouraging, Ben."

"I know, but you know how much I like math. I love to calculate the days in the school year," replied Ben. "Anyways, knowing how many days are left helps me to focus on summer break."

"Hmm, I see your point. If that helps the school year go faster for you, then I'm all in," Lizzy responded. "I'm keeping a positive attitude about this year!"

"That's the way to do it!" encouraged Ben. "Gotta go for now! See you tomorrow!"

"Okay, see you tomorrow," answered Lizzy. That was weird, thought Lizzy. Ben is being really nice to me lately. I wonder why?

As Lizzy entered the parking lot, she shaded her eyes from the bright sun. The scent of fresh blacktop was so strong that she crinkled her nose. She noticed that the heat was penetrating right through the soles of her shoes. As she neared her mom's car, she saw Kaylee climbing into her sister's B.M.W. Lizzy noticed that Ben was talking to Kaylee's older sister, Megan, while admiring her sports car.

"I wonder if he'll ask her for a ride," thought Lizzy.

Suddenly, Megan got into her car, slammed her driver's side door, and peeled out. Ben just stood there with a disappointed look on his face. I'm sure he wanted to go for a test drive in her car, thought Lizzy. Wow, it looks like Kaylee's sister is just like her. Poor Ben.

Lizzy soon spotted her mom and made her way to the car.

"Hi, Honey, how was your day?" asked Mom as Lizzy hopped into the front seat.

"It was okay," answered Lizzy. "We're one school day closer to Friday and the big game!"

"That reminds me," replied Mom, "I just called Jordan and Jenna's moms. They said it would be fine if we picked them up on our way to the game. We're going to leave around 6:30. Jenna's mom asked if you could spend the night, so if you'd like to, you can just pack your overnight bag and drop it at Jenna's when we pick her up."

"Cool! That will be so much fun!" exclaimed Lizzy emphatically. "I'll pack my bag tonight so I'm not too rushed on Friday! So.... what's for supper?" asked Lizzy.

"It's Tuesday," reminded Mom, "so it's your night to cook, remember?"

"Oh yeah," replied Lizzy. "I think I'm going to make... let me think...pancakes! We can put chocolate chips and whipped cream on top. My favorite!"

"Sounds wonderful!" replied Mom. "Let's plan on eating at 6:00, as usual."

"Alright," replied Lizzy. "I'm pretty sure I can have them done by then. Oh, and Mom, did you remember the popsicles when you went to the store today?"

"Of course," laughed Mom. "That's great!" responded Lizzy. "I'm so hungry for a cherry one. I think I could eat the whole box right now!"

CHAPTER 17

MAX!

"Do not give what is holy to dogs..."

T he minute Lizzy entered the house she made a bee-line for the kitchen freezer to get a popsicle.

"Hey Mom?" Lizzy asked after pulling the popsicle out of the box, "If you had to choose the best invention, what would it....Max!" scolded Lizzy as she battled the dog for her popsicle. "No! Give that back!" yelled Lizzy as Max took off with the popsicle in his mouth.

Lizzy chased Max around the kitchen table while Mom retrieved a doggie biscuit from the drawer. She called Max waving the biscuit in the air, and surprisingly, Max came toward the treat and dropped the popsicle on the floor.

"Well, at least it's still in the package, even though it's a little mangled," stated Lizzy breathlessly as she retrieved the popsicle from the floor. "I guess I'll put it in a bowl and eat it with a spoon. Thanks for helping me out, Mom. Hey, by the way, when will his trainer teach him to stop eating my food? This is really getting annoying!"

"We'll get there, Honey. Just be patient," responded

Mom. "The biggest mistake we made was feeding him food from the table. Now he prefers that over dog food. Eventually, he'll get used to eating only dog food, but that's going to take some time and a lot of consistency."

"I know," responded Lizzy, "I really love Max and I don't like to yell at him, but sometimes he makes me crazy!"

"I understand, Honey," replied Mom. "We just have to remember to be consistent with him, and follow all the rules his trainer has taught us. It's almost like our family is going to obedience school, not just Max! Maybe we should all learn to love doggie biscuits! They could become our new evening snack."

"You're funny, Mom!" laughed Lizzy. "But seriously, I'm really getting tired of eating snacks with millions of teeth marks in them. The last granola bar I wedged out of his mouth had fur all over it. I had to pick the hairs out of my mouth. It was so gross!" complained Lizzy dramatically.

"You should have just thrown it away, Lizzy," replied Mom. "You know that we have plenty more."

"I know," replied Lizzy, "but it was a chocolate peanut butter bar. You know that's my favorite! I couldn't stand to throw it away!"

"Oh, Lizzy! Life is never boring with you!" laughed Mom.

CHAPTER 18

Groceries on a Bike?

*...for consider how great of things
he has done for you...*

"So...what were you asking me before Max interrupted us and stole your popsicle?" Mom questioned.

"Oh, yeah," responded Lizzy, "if you had to choose the most important invention EVER... what would it be?"

"Hmm.... I'd have to think about that for a while," answered Mom. "Is this for a homework assignment or are you just curious?"

"It's for my science class," answered Lizzy. "We have to write a short paper and bring it in on Friday. Our assignment is to pick something that has had the biggest impact on the world and then explain why we chose that invention. Mr. Adams said we can get our parents' opinions, too. He's going to write all of our ideas on the whiteboard on Monday, and then we'll discuss them and choose the best one."

"That sounds like an interesting project," replied

Mom.

"That's what I thought," stated Lizzy." But I can't decide what it would be."

"What ideas have you come up with so far?" asked Mom.

"Well, I thought about cars, phones, and T.V.s," replied Lizzy. "But, I can't decide which one to pick... If people didn't have phones, they couldn't call each other or text. That would be just awful! But I guess you could just talk to people when you saw them. If you didn't have a car, you couldn't go very far. You'd have to ride your bike EVERYWHERE. How could you ever get groceries? Your popsicles would melt on the way home and you probably would have oranges rolling down the street!"

"Hmm," replied Mom. "Let's think about that. Was there any other form of transportation available before the invention of the automobile?"

"Um...trains, I guess, and horses!" answered Lizzy. "That would have been so cool to have your own horse!"

"Yes," replied Mom, "but owning a horse isn't as easy as most people think. So, people were able to travel without a car or bicycle. Are there any other inventions that you may have overlooked?"

"Let me see," pondered Lizzy.

"Let's think about our dinner tonight," suggested Mom. "How do you think people cooked pancakes before we had stoves like ours?"

"They had to light a fire in the bottom of the stove, like we saw at Sauder's Village. Oh, electricity!" exclaimed Lizzy. "That's a great idea! Without electricity, I couldn't cook dinner easily, charge my phone, listen to music, or even watch TV. Now that would be HORRIBLE!"

"You may be onto something there," said Mom.

"Yes, I bet that's the greatest invention ever!" exclaimed Lizzy excitedly. "Thanks for the help, Mom. I think that's the best answer! I'm going to get started writing my paper right now while it is fresh in my mind!"

Lizzy skipped to her room, happy to have finally chosen her invention!

CHAPTER 19

What a Good Dog, NOT!

*"But ask the animals and they
will teach you...."*

After writing her paper, Lizzy entered the kitchen and began gathering the supplies for her world famous pancakes. When she finished mixing the necessary ingredients, she slowly spooned small amounts of batter into the hot frying pan on the stove. When the pancakes were halfway cooked, she lifted one to flip it with the spatula. Suddenly, Max darted toward her while attempting to catch a fly. He jumped up and placed his front paws on the counter, tipping over the bowl of remaining pancake batter and bumping Lizzy's arm as she was flipping the pancake. Immediately, the half cooked pancake slid off the spatula and landed right on the top of Max's head!

"No, Max! Get down!" yelled Lizzy. "Mom, can you get Max out of here?" she called. "He jumped up while I was making my pancakes and now he has a pancake stuck to his head!"

Mom came running into the kitchen to get Max. Even though his dog collar was slippery, she was eventually able to get a good grip on him and lead him into the fenced-in backyard.

Lizzy wiped up the pancake batter on the counter and floor, and quickly went into her room to put on clean clothes. When she had finished changing, she smelled the distinct odor of burnt pancakes drifting into her bedroom. "Oh no!" she cried as she bolted toward the kitchen. The minute she entered the smoke-filled room, the piercing sound of the smoke detector rang out. Mom immediately ran into the kitchen to see if Lizzy needed help. As mom stood on a chair to fan the smoke away from the detector, Dad walked through the back door.

"Is everything alright?" Dad questioned as he entered the house.

"It is now," replied Mom after she got the alarm to stop ringing.

"What happened?" asked Dad as he walked into the kitchen. "I was afraid I was going to have to call the fire department!" he exclaimed as he waved his hands in front of him.

"It was just a little cooking mishap. We have everything under control now," answered Mom as she opened the kitchen windows to let some fresh air in.

"You need to scrub out the pan, and throw out the burnt pancakes Lizzy," instructed Mom. "Then you can turn the burner back on and finish cooking.

"Uh," hesitated Lizzy, "maybe I shouldn't cook anymore."

"Accidents happen, Honey, but you're doing fine," replied Mom. " I can't even count the number of times that I set off the smoke detector when I was learning to cook!

It's a good thing that your dad didn't mind chocolate chip cookies with a little black on the bottom of them!"

"Really?" asked Lizzy incredulously. "You're such a good cook, I can't believe you ever burnt anything!"

"That's how you learn, Kiddo," replied Dad as he glanced out the back window. "You're doing a great job, Lizzy. Don't let one little mishap discourage you from cooking....what's that on Max's head?"

"Oh, it's just a pancake... half cooked," mumbled Lizzy. "I'll give him a bath after dinner."

"I'm sure there's an interesting story behind this one," laughed Dad.

"There certainly is!" laughed Mom. "We'll explain it all at dinner."

After a short time, Lizzy called out, "It's time to eat!" She carried a large plate of pancakes to the table as her mom and dad took their seats around the table.

"Wow! Those look wonderful, Lizzy! I hope you have whipped cream to go with those, Kiddo! It's like icing on a cake," said Dad. "I'm starved!"

Lizzy's family talked and laughed about the day's events while they enjoyed their pancake dinner, forgetting about Max, as he miserably sat alone in the backyard.

CHAPTER 20

Thanks, Dad!

"I will wait for the Lord...."

After eating dinner, cleaning up the dishes andgiving Max a bath, Lizzy headed back to her room. Suddenly her phone chimed.

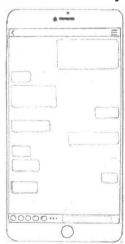

Jor: invention ideas?

Liz: all done.

Jor: no way!

Liz: any ides 4 u?

Jor: couple, not sure what 2 pick.

Liz: mine should win votes. sleepover's on.

Jor: yay, I'll bring my volleyball! lol

Liz: funny. hint...b4 u turn out lights, think of me!

Jor: electricity 1 of my choices.

Liz: awesome! ttyl

Jor: bye.

As Lizzy put her phone away, Dad knocked on her door.

"Hey, Kiddo . Those pancakes were fantastic! You're quite the cook!" Dad complimented.

"Thanks, Dad," replied Lizzy, "Maybe the next time I cook, I won't set off the smoke detector. But I'm glad you liked them. They're my favorite meal, next to meat loaf."

"Mine too," said Dad. "Hey, I never asked how school went today. Was it better than yesterday?"

"Other than falling off the stage during choir, it was a good day," lamented Lizzy.

"What! How did that happen?" asked Dad.

"Oh, we had to stand on the risers that are on the stage to practice our songs for the open house," explained Lizzy. "A bunch of girls behind me wanted to stand next to Kaylee, of course. Then, someone shoved Nikki and she fell into me, which forced me off the risers. I tried to catch my balance, but my foot went off the edge of the stage and SPLAT...just like Max's pancake!"

"Oh no," exclaimed Dad. "Are you alright?"

"Yeah, just a little embarrassed," Lizzy shared,

"What did the teacher say?" questioned Dad

"Well, she didn't really see what happened. She just asked if I was alright," said Lizzy.

"So, did you tell her what happened?" asked Dad.

"Not really, admitted Lizzy. "It wasn't like I got hurt physically or anything. Just a blow to my pride. If I got hurt, I would have said something."

"You know, Honey," replied Dad. "God wants us to be kind to others, but he doesn't expect us to be a walking mat for others to tromp on."

"I know, Dad," replied Lizzy. "But I did stand up for myself today, and it helped... at least for a while."

"Well, that's a start," said Dad. "You know, your mother and I pray for you every day. We hate to see you going through this."

"I know, Dad," said Lizzy. "I sure hope it gets better

soon."

"Me too, Kiddo, me too," stated Dad.

CHAPTER 21

Can't I Buy Happiness?

"For the love of money is the root of all evil..."

The evening passed quickly for Lizzy, and soon it was nearly bedtime. Lizzy entered the family room to tell her parents goodnight.

"Well, I'm heading to bed now," Lizzy said as she entered the room where her parents were sitting, both engrossed in their books.

"Goodnight, Honey," said Dad as he looked up from his book. "Hopefully you'll have a better day at school tomorrow. Are you sure you didn't get hurt from your fall off the stage today?"

"No, I'm fine, really," Lizzy answered.

"I'm sorry you had to experience that, Kiddo," stated Dad. "It's a shame the teacher didn't see what happened."

"Yeah," replied Lizzy. "But it was an accident. It could have happened to anyone."

"So, how much do you know about Kaylee?" asked Mom.

"All I know is that she's mean and she doesn't like me!"

exclaimed Lizzy. "She always gets straight A's and she's really rich, too! She wears new clothes ALL the time and has money to buy ice cream at school every day. She even lives in a mansion with an indoor pool! And, can you believe that she's got her own bathroom and a nanny?! Jenna said that she always gets to do whatever she wants, and to top it off, everyone wants to be her best friend!"

"Hmm...," replied Dad. "That sounds like she has a pretty nice life. But..., do you think she's happy?"

"Happy? Are you kidding? Why wouldn't she be? She's got everything she could ever want!" Lizzy answered.

"Well, material things don't necessarily buy happiness, Honey," replied Mom.

"Now you sound like Jenna!" Lizzy complained.

"Really?" asked Mom in a surprised tone.

"Yes," continued Lizzy. "She said that Kaylee's parents work all the time and Jenna's never even met them. She used to go to Kaylee's house all the time and has only seen her nanny and her sister, Megan."

"Well," advised Dad, "sometimes parents work a lot of hours to buy their children gifts to make them happy... when it's really the parents' time and attention that they want and need."

"Maybe she's mad about that and takes it out on you," added Mom.

"I don't know," said Lizzy. "I think if I had all the things she has, I'd be REALLY happy!"

"You know," said Dad, "there's a Bible verse I like to think of when I look at others and begin to want what they have... it's Hebrews 13:5. It says, 'Keep your eyes free from the love of money, and be content with what you have, for He has said I will never leave you or forsake you.'"

"Oh," mumbled Lizzy, "I've never heard that before."

"Well, it's a great verse to remember," said Dad. "It's actually one of my favorites. I know it's not always easy to have less than others, but everything we own is a gift from God. It's important to know that and try to have a thankful heart. It helps to keep us happy."

"Yeah, I guess that makes sense," replied Lizzy.

"Well, have a nice sleep, Kiddo," replied Dad.

"Thanks," replied Lizzy. "I love you guys."

"We love you, too," responded Mom. "We'll both be in later to kiss you goodnight!"

After brushing her teeth, Lizzy entered her bedroom and climbed into bed. She prayed:

"Dear Lord, thanks for today. Help me to be happy with what I have. Thanks for Mom and Dad. And...umm...help me to forgive Kaylee and...thanks for pancakes! Amen."

CHAPTER 22

Dance Away, Dance Away, Dance Away All!

"Be strong in the Lord..."

As the school year progressed, Lizzy settled into her school and study routine. Lizzy was happy that her invention idea for science class had received the highest number of votes. Kaylee continued to pick on Lizzy, but her attitude toward Kaylee had somehow begun to change. Lizzy found that her jealousy of Kaylee was slowly being replaced by a curiosity about Kaylee and her family. The greatest question she harbored in her mind was how often Kaylee even saw her parents. As Lizzy continued to pray daily for Kaylee, she began to gain a new understanding of her.

The weather was now in full winter mode, and Christmas time was quickly approaching. School was getting more challenging for Lizzy, too.

As Lizzy began another new day, she entered the school and made her way to her locker. She was surprised to see Ben already there waiting for her.

"Hey Lizzy," Ben said while leaning against her locker.

"Hi Ben," she answered.

"So…" he continued. "What's the difference between a rocking chair and a radio?"

"Um…I don't know…what?" said Lizzy.

"A rocking chair can only rock," answered Ben, "but a radio can rock and roll!"

Lizzy just smiled out of kindness at Ben's joke, which really wasn't very funny.

"Hi Lizzy. Hi Ben," Jordan called out as she walked to Lizzy's locker. "Are you at it again with your jokes, Ben?"

"Yep, always, and you missed a good one!" said Ben. "Don't you agree, Lizzy?"

"Uh…, yeah, it was kind of funny… I guess," replied Lizzy.

"Kind of funny….you guess?" asked Ben in astonishment. "Why doesn't anyone appreciate a good joke around here?"

"Hi Jenna," Lizzy and Jordan said in unison as Jenna approached Lizzy's locker.

"Hi," replied Jenna. "It feels like someone forgot to turn the furnace on in here; it's freezing! So what are you guys talking about?"

"Oh, Ben's just trying out his jokes on Lizzy again," laughed Jordan. "It must not have been a very good one because Lizzy didn't even laugh."

"Then you know it's bad, Ben," teased Jenna. "She laughs at everything!"

"No I don't!" Lizzy defended.

"Well… uh…I just like to try out my comedy on you guys. You know, perfection in presentation takes a lot of work!" defended Ben. "Hey, not to change the subject, but I was wondering if you guys are going to the winter dance next Friday? I heard a lot of people are going. Have you thought about it, Lizzy?"

"We've talked about it, but haven't decided for sure yet," responded Lizzy naively.

"Why do you ask, Ben?" replied Jordan with an ornery look in her eyes.

"Uh," stammered Ben, "I was just... wondering."

After an awkward silence, Ben continued,

"Oh boy, will you look at that time. I have to get to my locker before the bell rings. Bye guys... bye Lizzy." Ben smiled as he scurried away.

"Lizzy, he likes you!" squealed Jordan.

"No he doesn't," defended Lizzy, "he was just wondering if we were going to the dance," stated Lizzy.

"I heard a lot of people are going. Have you thought about it, Lizzy?" mocked Jenna.

"I know Ben, and I can tell he likes you!" accused Jordan while pointing her finger at Lizzy. "He's soooo cute!"

"Well, he's just a friend," responded Lizzy. "Anyways, I don't want a boyfriend yet. That would be weird. You have to spend lots of time together and act like you're all drooly over each other. Then if you ever break up, you're not friends anymore. Ben's a good friend- I wouldn't want to ruin that friendship."

"Yeah, good point," Jordan said while shrugging her shoulders.

"Hey are you guys going caroling with the choir Sunday afternoon?" asked Lizzy as they made their way to homeroom. She was glad to have changed the subject so quickly.

"I am," Jenna answered as they walked down the hall.

"Me, too," added Jordan.

"So am I," said Lizzy. "We're having hot chocolate and

cookies afterwards. I wouldn't want to miss that!"

"Oh Lizzy, you're funny," laughed Jenna. "The smallest things in life make you happy, especially if they involve food!"

"Well, it's good to be thankful for whatever we have," replied Lizzy.

"Yes, I suppose that's true," admitted Jordan. "Especially if it involves chocolate chip cookies!"

CHAPTER 23

Multiply!

"All hard work brings a profit…"

"**G**ood morning," Mrs. Wagner greeted her students after the bell rang. "I hope everyone had a great weekend. For those of you who are going caroling with the choir on Sunday, your permission slips need to be signed and turned in by this Thursday. Make sure you dress warmly, it's supposed to be cold this weekend. Also, tickets for the dance go on sale today in the office. Remember to follow the dress code rules that our school has set for the dance. Now, go make it a great day!"

As the students filed out of the classroom and headed to their first period class, Lizzy walked past Kaylee who was picking up her books from her locker.

"Hi Kaylee," Lizzy said as she walked by, catching her eye.

"Hi Lizard," Kaylee replied hesitantly.

As Lizzy and Jenna walked on to math class, Jordan caught up with them. "Why were you talking to her!" asked Jordan with disgust.

"I don't know," replied Lizzy, "I just thought I'd try to be nice to Kaylee and see what happens. I'm really getting tired of avoiding her."

"Well… it could work, but I wouldn't get my hopes up, Lizzy," responded Jordan. "Don't be surprised if she's still mean to you."

"You could be right," admitted Lizzy. "But, even if she is mean, I don't think it will bother me too much. It's kind of sad, but I think I've gotten used to it."

"Good morning class," Mr. Phillips impatiently barked out as the students entered math class. "I have your tests graded from Thursday and I'm sorry to say that we only had one A. Kaylee, great job. Keep up the good work! You are a real role model for your peers."

As Mr. Phillips passed back their tests, Lizzy's heart sank. One A and it had to be Kaylee, of course, thought Lizzy. And I studied so hard for that test!

"Lizzy," Mr. Phillips replied as he handed back her test. Lizzy spotted at the top of her paper a bright red C! Really, a C? thought Lizzy. I thought for sure I would have at least gotten a B on that test! I can't do anything right!

As class progressed, Lizzy felt her self esteem slowly deflating. She couldn't help but think how unfair life seemed. How could some people, like Kaylee, succeed in life without even trying? Why was school so difficult for her, while it came so easily for Kaylee? I'll never get good grades in math, she told herself.

About halfway through math class Mr. Phillips announced, "Alright class, please put your notebooks and pencils away. We're going to finish up our math class by playing Around the World with multiplication facts. This will give you all a chance to brush up on your skills. After all, multiplication is a very important part of mathematics. Jonathon, why don't you start us off. You'll start by challenging Becca, and whoever gives the correct answer to the multiplication fact first, gets to move on to challenge the next person. The slower person takes that student's seat. We'll see if anyone can make it around the entire classroom. Any questions? No?...then, let's get started."

Mr. Phillips quickly held up the fact card 9 x 9.

"81!" shouted Becca as Jonathon stood next to her.

"That's correct, Becca," stated Mr. Phillips. "Now, Jonathon, please take Becca's seat and Becca, you may move on to Emma."

The next fact card Mr. Phillips held up was 6 x 8.

"48," shouted Becca. Becca continued to move easily around the classroom. She was undefeated...until she got to Kaylee's desk.

The next challenge was 8 x 9.

"72!" Kaylee quickly shouted.

"That's correct, Kaylee," said Mr. Phillips. "Becca, I think Kaylee has broken your winning streak. Please take Kaylee's seat, and Kaylee, you may continue to Lizzy's desk."

Oh, great, thought Lizzy. Here Kaylee goes again, showing me up in front of the entire class. She lifted up a quick prayer.

Please, Lord, help me to do my best. Thanks!

"Oh, this next one is more difficult," Mr. Phillips stated as he held up 12 x 12.

"144!" shouted Lizzy, struggling to contain her excitement.

"You got it, Lizzy," replied Mr. Phillips. "You know the routine."

As the game progressed, Lizzy had the biggest winning

streak Mr. Phillips had seen this year. In fact, Lizzy was able to go around the entire classroom undefeated!

"Great job, Lizzy," Mr. Phillips congratulated. "I can tell you've worked hard on your multiplication facts. Since you set a new class record, I have a prize for you. You may have this pack of Skittles and a coupon to erase your worst grade. You may turn this coupon in at any time during this second quarter, so use it wisely."

"Thanks, Mr. Phillips!" Lizzy said happily. Inside, she was beaming with pride! This was the first time she'd surpassed Kaylee in anything! She had worked so hard over the summer on her multiplication facts, and it had definitely paid off! Suddenly, her C didn't seem so bad.

When the bell rang, Lizzy left math class with a newly found sense of confidence. She felt so excited. A compliment from Mr. Phillips was not easy to get! She was glowing!

CHAPTER 24

Really, Ben?

"Make a joyful noise unto the Lord..."

"**G**ood going, Lizzy!" Jenna said while giving Lizzy a high five as they exited the classroom.

"Yeah, that was so cool," crooned Jordan. "You actually beat Kaylee at something!"

"I know," replied Lizzy, with a big smile on her face.

"I can't believe it! I'll share my Skittles with you guys at lunch."

"That sounds good!" exclaimed Jordan.

As the girls entered the choir room, Lizzy noticed that a lot of Kaylee's friends were suddenly being nice to HER instead of Kaylee.

That's strange, thought Lizzy. I wonder why everyone is being so nice. They probably just want some of my candy.

"Hey, Lizzy," said Ben as she was ready to take her seat. "Great going in math!"

"Thanks," smiled Lizzy.

"I have a good one for you," continued Ben. "What has four wheels and flies?"

"Um... I don't know... what?" asked Lizzy curiously.

"A garbage truck, of course!" laughed Ben.

"Oh boy," Lizzy mumbled.

"Good morning class," greeted Mrs. Hobner as everyone was seated.

Once again, people were quietly chuckling at Mrs. Hobner's appearance. Her purple framed glasses had somehow become bent and were sitting at an angle on her nose. Her bright purple pants came just above her ankles, leaving just enough room to reveal her mismatched socks. One sock was red with black roses and the other was pink with purple polka dots. Her bright red and blue striped shirt looked ghastly next to her bright purple pants!

I seriously wonder if she gets dressed in the dark, Lizzy thought once again.

"Good morning, it's nice to seeee-eeee all of you again," sang Mrs. Hobner. "I hope all of you are planning to go car-o-ling this Sunday. Remember that we're meeting in the Community Room at the White Pines Nursing Home. Your parents may join us there if they would like. Also, by participating in this joyous event, you will earn ex-tra credit points," she sang. "It will be a de-la-la-lightful, de-la-la-lovely experience! Oh my golly, I see a hand raised, Kaylee did you have a question?"

"Yes," Kaylee replied in her sweetest voice. "I can go caroling, but I don't have any way to get to the nursing home. My parents are in Europe, my sister has plans, and it's my nanny's day off."

"Hey, Kaylee," joked Ben. "Tell your sister that if my brother and I can drive her car, we'd be happy to take you there."

"Funny, Ben," Kaylee snarled.

"I think carpooling for this event is a won-der-ful idea!" sang Mrs. Hobner. "Would any of you be willing to offer Kaylee transportation?"

Everyone sat silently in their chairs looking down. After noticing that there were no volunteers, Lizzy hesitantly raised her hand.

"We could pick you up, Kaylee," Lizzy meekly offered.

Lizzy's classmates seemed dumbfounded. It was so quiet in the room, you could have heard a pin drop! She couldn't believe the looks on her classmates' faces. One girl even had her mouth open!

"Well, isn't that nice," sang Mrs Hobner. "It looks like you can go car-o-ling after all, Kaylee. Just touch base with Lizzy, and give her your address. Then she can Map Seek or Gooble the directions, or whatever you call it. Good heavens, we've wasted so much class time flapping our jaws. Let's begin warming up our voices by singing the scales....Now where did I put that tuner?"

CHAPTER 25

What a Mouthful!

"Blessed are the peacemakers..."

Before Lizzy knew it, lunchtime had arrived. As Lizzy entered the cafeteria, she saw Kaylee carrying her lunch tray heading toward her friends. As Kaylee sat down beside Kristin, Becca and Emma, the three girls suddenly got up carrying their lunches and moved to a different table, far away from Kaylee. Lizzy noticed a surprised and dejected look on Kaylee's face that she had never seen before.

Wow, thought Lizzy. I wonder what Kaylee did to make everyone so mad. As Lizzy was looking for a place to sit, she felt a gentle nudging from her conscience. I think I'm going to sit by Kaylee, thought Lizzy. I'd feel terrible if no one wanted to sit by me!

"Hi, Kaylee, can I sit here?" asked Lizzy as she approached Kaylee.

"It's a free country," mumbled Kaylee.

Lizzy sat down directly across from Kaylee. As Lizzy looked up, she saw Jordan and Jenna standing behind Kaylee a couple of tables away. Their eyes were as big as saucers. Jordan started shaking her head at Lizzy and pointing to a different table. But, Lizzy just smiled at them. Eventually, Jordan and Jenna sheepishly joined Lizzy at her table. After a very awkward silence, Jordan finally spoke.

"So...," Jordan replied.

"So....what?" asked Lizzy cheerily.

"Um...it sure is cold out," Jenna stated.

"Yep," added Kaylee while looking at her food.

"Hey, thanks for giving me a ride to White Pines, Lizard," said Kaylee as she continued looking down.

"Oh, it's no problem," Lizzy replied. "Um...Ben sure likes your sister's car, don't you think, Kaylee?"

"Yeah," Kaylee answered. "He keeps trying to talk her into giving him a ride in it, but she won't give anyone a ride unless it's a good friend."

"But he's YOUR friend, isn't he...kind of?" asked Lizzy meekly.

"He just likes nice cars," Kaylee barked. "A lot of people are like that. They're your best friend if you have something they want."

Oh...," replied Lizzy uncomfortably. "Anyways..., what's going on with your friends, Kaylee? It seems like they're mad about something."

"They're just being stupid," answered Kaylee. "They'll get over it."

"Uh... what are you wearing when we go caroling, Jordan?" asked Jenna, carefully trying to change the subject.

"I'm just wearing jeans and my new boots. They're really warm and comfy. What are you wearing?" asked Jordan.

"Well, it's obviously too cold to wear a dress!" barked Kaylee. "So, I'm sure she'll wear jeans."

"I wasn't asking if she was going to wear a dress!" defended Jordan.

"Okay, Jordan, chill! I got it!" barked Kaylee.

"Hey, there's no reason to get mad," defended Lizzy. "Jordan was just wondering if she should wear jeans or nicer pants, weren't you, Jordo?"

"Yep," mumbled Jordan as she looked away and took another bite of her lunch.

"And you're probably just upset because of your friends, Kaylee," continued Lizzy. "I'm sure it wasn't anything personal against Jordo, right Kaylee?"

"Yeah," conceded Kaylee. "Sorry I raised my voice, Jordan."

"That's alright," replied Jordan quietly.

"It should be fun caroling," continued Lizzy. "And with your voice, Kaylee, it'll help our group sound better... right Jordo?"

"Yeah..., I guess," grunted Jordan.

"Hey, are you going to eat that muffin, Jenna?" asked Lizzy while eyeing Jenna's lunchbox.

"Nope, you can have it, Lizzy," answered Jenna, "I'm stuffed!"

"Thanks!" answered Lizzy with a gleam in her eye.

"Wow, would you look at the time!" said Jenna.

"We only have a couple minutes left," Jordan added.

"Are you ready, Lizzy?"

"Almmmooosth," Lizzy attempted to answer with her mouth full of food.

"What was that?" asked Jenna.

Suddenly the girls started laughing, as Lizzy took one last swallow of her milk to wash down her muffin.

"I have to admit," laughed Kaylee, "you are funny, Lizard!"

"Let's move it," said Jordan. "I don't want to be late for science."

"Alright, now I'm ready!" Lizzy said while wiping her mouth on her sleeve and popping up from her seat.

"Bye, Kaylee," said Lizzy as she turned and walked away with her friends..

"Bye, Lizard," mumbled Kaylee.

CHAPTER 26

Scheming? Who's Scheming?

*"Do unto others as you wish that
others would do to you..."*

"**L**izzy, why did you sit by HER?" scolded Jordan, as the three girls walked towards their lockers.

"I felt bad for her having to eat all by herself," defended Lizzy.

"Well, she probably deserved it," added Jenna. "That's one thing about you, Lizzy. You're always thinking of others. Except when there's food involved...then you get distracted!"

"What!" Lizzy shot back.

"I'm just teasing!" laughed Jenna.

"I just hope Kaylee makes up with her friends soon," groaned Jordan. "I'd hate to have to go through that again!"

"Me too!" added Jenna adamantly. "Don't you agree, Lizzy?"

"Hmm?" Lizzy answered absentmindedly.

"Oh no, I know that look," accused Jordan. "What are you scheming, Lizzy?"

"Me, scheming?" defended Lizzy.

"Yes! You're going to find a way to get Kaylee and her friends back together," accused Jordan. "I know you too well, Lizzy!"

"Well, now that you mention it," said Lizzy, "that IS a very good idea."

"Lizzy, maybe you should just leave it alone," warned Jenna. "She's really mean. I don't want to see you get hurt anymore by her."

"I know," replied Lizzy. "But sometimes you just have to do the right thing, because....it's the right thing to do. I've been praying for Kaylee, and I think God wants me to try to be nice to her. Anyways, how else will she know that I have God's love in my heart if I don't show it?"

"I'm not so sure about this, Lizzy," warned Jordan. "It might backfire on you."

"So,.... do you have a plan?" questioned Jenna hesitantly.

"Not yet," replied Lizzy, "but when I do, you two will be the first to know. Anyways, I might need your help."

"Hey, Lizzy," interrupted Ben as he joined Lizzy's group on their way to science class. "Why did the chicken walk on the road?"

"To get to the other side?" asked Lizzy curiously.

"Nope, because the sidewalk ended! Gotcha again!" Ben laughed.

"Ohhh," moaned Lizzy. "Well, I have to admit that your jokes are getting better."

"I know," replied Ben. "I'm working on some new material. Get ready for the new and improved Ben!"

CHAPTER 27

Sor-HIC!-ry

"A cheerful heart is good medicine..."

"Good afternoon class," said Mr. Adams as the students filed into the science room and took their seats. "I hope you all have full stomachs and are ready to learn."

Suddenly, Lizzy let out a loud hiccup. She put her hand over her mouth with a surprised look on her face. Some of her classmates started chuckling, and Mr. Adams looked at her with a smile on his face.

"You probably ate that muffin too fast," whispered Jordan.

"Sor-HIC-ry," Lizzy said to Mr. Adams.

"Would you like to get a drink of water from the drinking fountain, Lizzy?" asked Mr. Adams.

"O-HIC-kay, answered Lizzy as she quickly got up and bolted toward the hallway.

"HIC!...oh no, I got water up my nose," Lizzy moaned loudly at the drinking fountain. She had no idea how loudly her voice carried through the hallway. Suddenly everyone in her class burst out laughing, including Mr. Adams. As Lizzy entered the classroom, she was still hiccuping.

"Please open your books to Chapter 9 beginning on page 115," instructed Mr. Adams.

Every time Lizzy hiccupped, the class began laughing,

including Lizzy. It was so refreshing for Lizzy to finally laugh at herself, rather than feeling embarrassed or being critical of herself. After about ten minutes, her hiccups finally stopped. As Lizzy daydreamed in class, she thought about how her confidence had started to grow. She had a great family and friends who cared for her and had her back. It was a great feeling! She was beginning to realize and appreciate the many ways that God had blessed her life.

And, with no more distractions, science class flew by.

CHAPTER 28

Aha!

"The plans of the diligent..."

"How's your journaling going, Lizzy?" asked Jordan while the trio walked together to language arts class.

"My notebook's almost full," admitted Lizzy. "Mom's taking me to buy another one after school today."

"Wow," moaned Jordan. "I haven't written that much in mine."

"Me either," said Jenna. "You must really like to write."

"I sure do!" said Lizzy. "Mrs. Weichers said my writing shows that I have a compassionate heart, whatever that means."

"That means you care about other people's feelings," answered Jordan. "That's why you sat by Kaylee at lunchtime. Even though she's mean to you, you still care about her feelings."

"Well," added Lizzy, "I felt bad for her, that's all."

As the girls entered language arts class, Lizzy noticed that Kaylee was still alone. It was the strangest thing. None of the girls were speaking to her. It was as if she were invisible. As Lizzy turned to take her seat, she noticed Ben look at her and smile.

Oh boy, thought Lizzy, maybe Jordan was right. I think he DOES have a crush on me.

As she returned a half smile, she wondered how she was going to let Ben down gently without hurting their friendship.

"Good afternoon everyone," greeted Mrs. Weichers. "I'd like each of you to be brainstorming a topic for your Opinion Essay. Remember that it needs to be your opinion, although you are required to include facts that support your opinion. It must be typed, at least two pages, and it will be due on January 7th. That's the first Friday after Christmas break. I will also give extra credit to anyone who would like to read their essay orally to the class. It will be great practice for public speaking."

As Lizzy was listening to Mrs. Weichers, she noticed Kaylee and Brent exchange a glance and smile at each other.

"Oh! Now I get it!" Lizzy exclaimed louder than she had meant to.

"Did you have something to say, Lizzy?" asked Mrs. Weichers.

"Oh....no....I was just thinking," she stammered.

"Alright, let's try to keep our thoughts to ourselves until class is over," instructed Mrs. Weichers.

"Sorry," replied Lizzy meekly. I can't believe I figured it out, thought Lizzy. I can't wait to tell Jordo and Jenna!

When class was over, Lizzy was beaming. "I know why everyone's mad at Kaylee!" Lizzy exclaimed to Jordan and Jenna as they were walking to their lockers.

"Why?" Jordan and Jenna asked in unison.

"Meet me at my locker after school," instructed Lizzy. "I'll explain everything then. I finally have a plan!"

"Oh, no!" Jordan and Jenna moaned in unison.

CHAPTER 29

Initiate Plan BEKK

"Strive for peace with everyone..."

After computer class was over, Jordan and Jenna reached Lizzy's locker with anxious looks on their faces.

"So...why is everyone so mad at Kaylee, and what's your big plan?" asked Jenna excitedly.

"Yeah!" exclaimed Jordan. "You've kept us in suspense all of eighth period. Throw us a bone here!"

"Well," whispered Lizzy, "you know how Kristin likes Brent, right?"

"Everyone knows that!" stated Jordan matter-of-factly.

"But...," revealed Lizzy, "I'll bet you didn't know that KAYLEE likes Brent and he likes HER!"

"No way!" exclaimed Jordan. "Who told you that?"

"I saw Kaylee smile at Brent, and he smiled back!" Lizzy stated sneakily.

"So, they smiled at each other," stated Jordan. "A lot of people smile at each other, Lizzy. What's the big deal?"

"That's true," agreed Jenna.

"But," added Lizzy, "Kaylee and Brent smiled at each other the same way that Ben smiles at me."

"I told you Ben likes you, Lizzy!" accused Jordan.

"Well, it was pretty obvious to me today," conceded Lizzy. "You guys were right about Ben all along."

"Of course, we're ALWAYS right!" teased Jordan.

"Very funny," laughed Lizzy.

"I can't believe Kaylee and Brent like each other!" exclaimed Jenna.

"Yeah," added Jordan. "No wonder none of the girls are talking to Kaylee. It all makes sense now. Kristin has been telling everyone for months how much she likes Brent!"

"I know!" agreed Jenna. "I can't believe Kaylee would go for someone that her best friend likes so much!"

"So...," continued Lizzy, "that's why I have a plan."

"Oh, I don't know if I'm going to like this," groaned Jordan.

Jordan and Jenna listened intently as Lizzy explained her big plan.

"Tomorrow morning before school starts," continued Lizzy, "we'll casually walk by Kristin's locker when Becca and Emma are there. You know how Becca loves to eavesdrop on everyone's conversations?" asked Lizzy.

"Yes!...," both girls answered in unison.

"And then she tells everyone what she's heard," complained Jordan.

Well...," continued Lizzy, "we'll stop near her locker and talk loud enough so they can hear us, of course. I'll mention to you that there's someone that wants to go out with me. Then I'll say that I just don't want a boyfriend yet. I'll give you a bunch of reasons why it doesn't make sense to be in a relationship right now. I'll make sure to mention that when you break up, because you always do, you've lost a friend. And it's not worth risking a friendship. I'll also mention that I'm having too much fun with you guys and that I don't want to give up my time hanging out with you. Then you can add anything you want to agree with me."

The girls came up with many reasons why they would rather spend time with their friends, than with a boy.

"Then," added Lizzy, "I'll finish by saying that I would never want to ruin my friendship with you two because of a guy! That would just be stupid!"

"I have to admit, Lizzy," admitted Jenna incredulously, this just might work!"

"I sure hope so," added Jordan.

"So," added Lizzy, "tomorrow we initiate plan BEKK."

"BEKK?" asked Jordan. "What does that mean?"

"Becca...B, Emma...E, Kristin...K, and of course, Kaylee...K," stated Lizzy, "BEKK."

"I get it!" exclaimed Jenna. "We're trying to bring them back together, so BEKK it is!"

"Got it," replied Jordan. "Plan BEKK will begin tomorrow!"

CHAPTER 30

I've Got an Idea!

*"...clothe yourselves with com-
passion, kindness..."*

Soon, the school day was over and it was time to pack up to go home. Lizzy bundled up in her coat, scarf, and gloves, slung her backpack on, and quickly proceeded to the parent pick up point. As she climbed into the family car, Mom greeted her, "Hi Honey. How was your day?"

"Good," answered Lizzy as she put her face in front of the vent blowing out warm air. "I'm freezing! It's so cold in the school, I don't think the furnace is working right. At least it feels good in here! So... what's for dinner, I'm starving!"

"Chicken Rice casserole," replied Mom.

"Yum!" exclaimed Lizzy. "Did you put lots of broccoli and cheese in it?" Lizzy asked hopefully.

"I sure did," answered Mom. "I made it just the way you like it."

"Awesome!" crooned Lizzy. "Oh Mom, would it be alright if we picked up Kaylee on our way to White Pines Nursing Home on Sunday?"

"Kaylee? As in the Kaylee who calls you a lizard?" inquired Mom.

"Yes," said Lizzy meekly. "She doesn't have a ride for caroling, and no one would volunteer to take her, so...I did. I hope that's alright?" Lizzy questioned hesitantly.

"Of course it's alright," said Mom. "If someone is in need and you want to help out, that's a good thing. As long as you don't get hurt in the process."

"I know, Mom," Lizzy responded quietly.

"What made you offer to give her a ride? Has something changed between the two of you girls?" asked Mom.

"No, nothing really," replied Lizzy. "I've just been thinking about what Dad said. He wondered if Kaylee was even happy. Jenna said Kaylee almost never sees her parents, so I kind of feel sorry for her."

"Well, Honey," said Mom, "I'm very proud of you for stepping up to help. I think my little girl is growing up."

"Oh, Mom, I haven't been little for a long time," defended Lizzy.

"I know," said Mom, "but you'll always be my little girl, no matter how old you get. Now, let's go get that journal, so you can continue your writing," said Mom.

"Okay, but just don't call me your little girl in front of anyone, PLEASE?" pleaded Lizzy.

"You got it! I won't say it aloud, but inside I'll still be thinking it!" smiled Mom.

When Lizzy and Mom finished up in the store they drove home. As they entered their house, Max greeted Lizzy with a sloppy kiss on her face. "Hi Max!" Lizzy said as she patted Max on his head. "I missed you, too!" She quickly checked out the casserole in the oven and then opened the kitchen drawer and took out a doggie biscuit for Max.

While he happily ate his treat, Lizzy grabbed an apple out of the fruit bowl on the counter, and headed to her room to start her homework.

Soon Lizzy's phone vibrated with a text message.

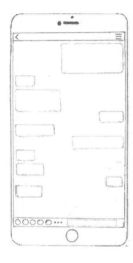

Ben: "hey going to dance?"

Liz: "yep with jordo n jenna"

Ben: "want 2 meet?"

Liz: "uh... will c u n everyone else there"

Ben: "ok c u then"

Liz: "c ya"

Oh boy, thought Lizzy, I was hoping that if I didn't encourage him, he'd give up on me. Now I'm going to have to tell him that I just want to be friends. He's a really nice guy...Wait a minute, I have an idea.

Oh, this is great, Lizzy thought ex - citedly.

CHAPTER 31

Ten Reasons Why

"Do not be conformed to this world..."

After Lizzy finished her homework, she began to write her opinion essay. The words just seemed to flow. She could think of numerous reasons and found many facts to support the benefits of waiting until you're older to date. Since she had very strong feelings about her topic, she found it a very easy paper to write. I can't believe I almost have two pages done, thought Lizzy excitedly. Maybe Mrs. Weichers will let me read it to the class tomorrow. That way, I can get extra credit and remain friends with Ben without hurting his feelings.

Before Lizzy knew it, Mom called her to dinner. To Lizzy's surprise, Max calmly sat next to the table and was very well behaved during the meal. They had learned from their dog trainer to give Max a doggie treat before the family meals. If he didn't swipe any food from the table, he would receive another treat after the meal. Max was finally beginning to understand the concept of obedience and looked forward to his treats. After helping to clean up the kitchen after dinner, Lizzy headed to her room. As she entered her room, she heard her phone chime, notifying her of a text.

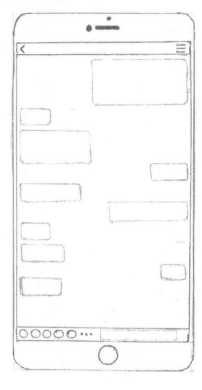

Jord: ideas 4 essay?

Liz: just about finished

Jord: no way! what about?

Liz: 10 reasons y it's better 2 wait 2 date

Jord: seriously?

Liz: yep n it might help with r plan

Jord: how?

Liz: will explain at school. u have a topic yet?

Jord: still thinking

Liz: hope you get one soon...need help?

Jord: will let you know

Liz: ok c u tom

Jord: ttyl

Liz: bye

Lizzy was getting tired as she finished her paper and decided to go to bed. She went to the family room to tell her parents goodnight.

"Hey, Kiddo," said Dad, "your mom mentioned that you're picking up Kaylee for caroling on Sunday."

"Yeah," Lizzy replied as she shrugged her shoulders. "She needed a ride."

"That's a very thoughtful thing that you're doing, Honey," commented Dad. "It's not always easy putting someone else's needs before your own."

"I know," replied Lizzy. "But since I've been praying for Kaylee, it's been easier to forgive her."

"It seems as though your prayer is being answered in a different way than any of us would have thought," replied Dad. "God works in mysterious ways."

"He sure does!" added Lizzy.

"And you have a very compassionate heart," stated Mom. "That's another reason why we're so proud of you."

"That's what Mrs. Weichers wrote in my journal!" said Lizzy in a surprised tone.

"Just keep up the good work and keep praying for Kaylee. We're praying for her also," added Dad. "Well, it's getting late, Honey. You'd better head to bed now. Have a nice sleep. We love you."

"I love you, too," she replied. "Goodnight."

Before Lizzy turned out the lights, she prayed:

"Dear Lord, thanks for my family. Help Kaylee to get back together with her friends and to see your love in me. Umm.... please forgive me for my sins, help Jordo with her dad, and thanks for chicken rice casseroles! Amen."

As Lizzy drifted off to sleep, she recalled the verse in Colossians 3:12

"Therefore, as God's chosen people, holy and dearly loved, clothe yourselves with compassion, kindness, humility, gentleness and patience."

CHAPTER 32

Success!

*"But always strive to do what is
good for each other..."*

The following day in language arts class, Lizzy was given permission to read her essay to the class. As she made her way to the front of the room, she could feel her heart beating rapidly, and her knees shaking. As she attempted to speak, her voice squeaked loudly. Some of the boys began laughing as Jonathon accused her of swallowing a lizard. But surprisingly, Kaylee spoke up in Lizzy's defense. Once she began reading, her knees quit shaking and her voice remained within her normal pitch. She was able to speak with passion while holding the interest of her classmates. Ben sat at his desk with a funny look on his face. He now knew that it would be pointless to pursue a relationship with Lizzy at this time. But he was determined that someday, when they were older, he was going to date her. For now, they would continue to be good friends.

The girl's plan, along with Lizzy's essay, got some of

the girls in her class thinking. By the end of the school day, Kaylee and Kristin were once again speaking to each other. Lizzy overheard Kaylee tell Kristin that she wouldn't ruin their friendship just because of Brent. But Kristin decided that it didn't make sense to like someone who didn't like her in return. It was actually nice for Lizzy to see the girls back together.

Finally, the night of caroling arrived. Lizzy picked up Kaylee as planned, and Kaylee was surprisingly pleasant to Lizzy. Lizzy was stunned to find Kaylee slip up at one point and call her Lizzy, rather than Lizard, while speaking to her. She wondered if this could be the beginning of a better relationship, or if Kaylee would fall back into her old habits of name calling and bullying. Lizzy wasn't quite sure what to make of Kaylee's new attitude, but she liked it. Perhaps someday they could even become friends. Only time would tell.

Everyone had a great time caroling with their friends. The highlight of the night for Lizzy, of course, were the cookies and hot chocolate!

When the following weekend arrived, everyone was excited for the dance. Lizzy and her friends had a great time dancing and hanging out with their classmates! Lizzy was afraid that Ben might try to avoid her, since everyone was talking about her essay. But just the opposite had happened. He seemed to have gained a new respect for her. Lizzy was impressed by his mature attitude. Maybe someday, she thought, they might become more than just friends...but not just yet!

CHAPTER 33

I Love This Time of Year!

"For God so loved the world..."

Before Lizzy knew it, Christmas break had arrived. Lizzy loved this time of year. The lights on the homes throughout their small town, along with the joy of the season, warmed Lizzy's heart. She cherished the time that she and her dad spent together shopping for that special gift for her mom every year. After shopping, she and Dad would go out to eat at Lizzy's favorite restaurant. She enjoyed spending time with her cousins and sleeping in on the dark, cold mornings. Her parents had surprised her with a trip to her grandparents' house in Tennessee. It was a long drive, but she was so excited to spend time with her grandparents, whom she hadn't seen in nearly a year. She had a wonderful time with her family, and hated to leave. But she was anxious to get back home to see Max, who had spent the week at Golden Paws Kennel. Christmas break flew by for Lizzy. She was sad to see it end, but she was looking forward to seeing her friends once again at school. Lizzy felt refreshed and ready to take on the second half of the school year. As her mom dropped her off on a dark, sleepy morning, Lizzy quickly ran into the school to get out of the frigid air. As she entered the building out of breath, she spotted Ben.

Hey Lizzy," said Ben. "How was your break?"

"It was great! I'll tell you all about it at recess," replied Lizzy happily.

"How was yours?" she asked.

"Oh, I had a nice time, and I came up with some more jokes, like I said I would," Ben boasted. "So, Lizzy," asked Ben, ... what did the saw say to the wood?"

"I don't know," laughed Lizzy... "what?"

"Wood it be okay if I saw you tomorrow?" laughed Ben. "Get it? wood...saw."

Oh boy," chuckled Lizzy

"So, that was a little bit funny?" asked Ben.

"Yeah, you made me laugh!" conceded Lizzy. "It was funny."

"Yes!" Ben said as he raised his fist in triumph. Soon Jordan and Jenna met up with Lizzy and Ben at Lizzy's locker. As the group headed to homeroom together, Lizzy noticed Ben looking at her with a half smile on his face. It seemed like their friendship had grown stronger than before Christmas break!

CHAPTER 34

What's a Legacy?

*"The integrity of the upright
guides them…"*

After the announcements in homeroom, the students were asked to quickly share with the class their favorite part of Christmas break. Lizzy excitedly told the class about her surprise trip to her grandparents' home in Tennessee. It was great fun hearing about everyone's Christmas breaks! Kaylee opened up and talked about spending time with her family. Lizzy was happy to hear that even Kaylee had a nice time with her family.

The morning seemed to fly by, especially since everyone seemed happy to see their friends once again after the break. Before Lizzy knew it, lunchtime had arrived.

"I'll hurry and save seats," Lizzy told her friends as she grabbed her lunch box from her locker.

"See you there," said Jordan as she and Jenna walked to the lunch line. As Lizzy sat down in the cafeteria, she noticed Kaylee sitting on the other end of the table with her old group of friends. They were getting along so well together that no one would have guessed that Kaylee had been at odds with her friends before Christmas break. Just then, Jordan and Jenna joined Lizzy at the table.

"So, what did you pack for lunch today, Lizzy?" asked Jenna.

"I have a ham sandwich, chips, a cheese stick, some peanuts.... an apple...cucumber slices, um...juice and a cookie."

"How can you eat all that?" asked Jordan incredulously.

"I guess I'm just hungry," replied Lizzy.

"You're always hungry," laughed Jenna.

"That's the biggest understatement of the year!" added Jordan.

"Hey are you guys ready to dissect an earthworm in science class today?" asked Jordan with a mischievous look on her face. "You might not want to eat so much, Lizzy. You might ralph!"

"I don't even want to think about that," moaned Jenna, as she pushed the rest of her food away.

"I think it'll be pretty cool!" continued Jordan. "We can see what the inside of an earthworm looks like. Did you know that your blood is actually blue in your veins but once it hits oxygen, it turns red? I wonder if it's the same for worms."

"Oh, please stop, Jordo!" complained Jenna. "I've just lost my appetite."

"If you're so excited about this disgusting science project, then you can do the dissecting in our group," replied Jenna.

"That sounds like a plan," agreed Jordan.

As the girls were finishing their lunch, Lizzy eyed Jenna's food.

"Hey, are you going to eat that candybar, Jenna?" asked Lizzy sheepishly.

"No, Lizzy," replied Jenna, "it's all yours. I think I'm feeling sick already!"

"Well, I don't want to think about earthworms while I'm eating," laughed Lizzy. "Right now I'm just trying to focus on my food...and enjoy it."

"Like always!" laughed Jordan.

"Speaking of focusing," whispered Jenna. "Did you notice the girls at the end of the table? It looks like Kaylee and Kristin are best friends again. Your plan seems to have worked, Lizzy!"

"Yeah," agreed Jordan. "That was a great idea, Lizzy. And I can't believe you got up in front of the whole class and read your essay!"

"I know!" agreed Jenna. "Did you see Ben's face? He looked so uncomfortable."

"I know he did," added Jordan. "But he seems fine with it now. He's still a great friend to you, Lizzy, as always. You even got some of the girls in class rethinking the whole dating idea."

"Well, I just want to make sure I leave a good legacy," replied Lizzy. "That's really important to me."

"What's a legacy?" asked Jordan with a confused look on her face. "And why have you been using all these strange words today, Lizzy?"

"Well," replied Lizzy, "Mom and Dad got me this calendar for Christmas which teaches a new word and its definition each day. I try to add the words to my daily vocabulary. Dad and I play this little game. I try to randomly use the word in a sentence to see if he knows what I'm talking about. He hates it when I know the meaning of a word that he doesn't know," she laughed. "Anyways, today's word is

LEGACY. One definitions is, 'Something handed down from one generation to the next.' It says that someone can leave a legacy of honesty and integrity. So I've decided to try to leave a legacy of compassion and contentment."

"Hey, that's pretty cool, Lizzy," replied Jenna.

"Leave it to you to think that one up," said Jordan. "I'm sure you'll do it, too. Hey, you'd better hurry and shove the rest of that candybar in your mouth, Lizzy, it's time to go dissect an earthworm!"

"Yuck!" replied Lizzy and Jenna in unison.

CHAPTER 35

Wasn't That Cool!

"He will yet fill your mouth with laughter..."

As Lizzy and her friends entered the science lab, they noticed the overpowering smell of formaldehyde. Lizzy wrinkled her nose, while many of the girls in the class complained about the smell. Jordan, on the other hand, had a look of great anticipation on her face, which was matched by most of the boys in the classroom. After taking their seats, Mr. Adams gave directions about the dissection and told them the parts of the earthworm they would be identifying and labeling on their worksheets. As he passed out one worm to each group, Ben started in with his jokes.

"Hey, Lizzy," replied Ben, "my earthworm was very humble. Do you know why?"

"No...," answered Lizzy hesitantly, "why?"

"Because, he was very down to earth. Get it? Down to earth."

"Oh boy, Ben," mumbled Jenna as she fanned her face.

"Hey, that was a good one," replied Ben. "Didn't you think so, Lizzy?" Ben said while smiling at Lizzy.

"I think it's funny that all the girls in here, except

Jordan, of course, are grossed out by these worms, and here you are, Ben, making worm jokes!" laughed Lizzy.

"Well, what can I say?" asked Ben. "I just see the humor in lots of things."

Ben's upbeat attitude soon spread throughout the entire classroom. Before the period was halfway over, every group had given their worm a name and identified its personality. Most of the boys were pretending their worms were having conversations with each other. Mr. Adams didn't seem to mind, as it lightened the mood. It was never easy to get girls interested in dissecting anything, unless it was a plant. Soon the whole class was laughing and joining in with the jokes. It was hard for Mr. Adams to keep a straight face as he had the students identify the parts of the earthworm.

When science class was ending, the girls cleaned up their tables, threw away their gloves, and made a beeline for the restroom to wash their hands.

"Wasn't that cool?" asked Jordan as they walked to their lockers.

"Yeah," replied Lizzy. "It's cool that it's over with! That smell was SO disgusting!"

"I hope we never have to do that again," moaned Jenna.

"I'm sorry to tell you this, Jenna, but in eighth grade we dissect frogs!" laughed Jordan.

"Oh no!" groaned Lizzy and Jenna in unison.

CHAPTER 36

A Surprise?

*"God is a God of fresh starts and
new beginnings…"*

As time went by, Lizzy was excited to see the season change from the cold, dreariness of winter to the freshness and excitement of spring. She loved the warmer weather with the brighter days and extended daylight hours. Along with the springtime came many school activities, with the highlight being the school's spring choir concert. Mrs. Hobner outdid herself with her most outlandish clothes yet. Some of the parents in the audience believed her attire was a costume designed for the concert. Her pink and purple frilly sundress was complemented by green and black knee high argyle socks. She wore black army boots along with a large straw hat with plastic birds sitting in a nest. It was quite a comical sight. No one in the audience took her seriously until the choir began to sing. By the end of the concert, the choir received a standing ovation, with Mrs. Hobner gaining a new respect from the students and members of the audience alike. She had taken the choir to a new level of singing that everyone seemed very proud of.

Kaylee still picked on Lizzy but it happened less frequently and in a less hurtful way. Lizzy was beginning to realize the importance of praying for others, and the impact that her actions had on others. Even amidst the many struggles that Lizzy faced during the sixth grade, she was noticing some positive results from her obedience to the Lord.

Finally, with much anticipation, the last day of the school year had arrived.

"Hey, Lizzy," Ben said as he joined her at her locker.

"Hi, Ben," she replied as she smiled at him.

"So.....what did the boat say to the anchor?" he asked.

"I don't know...what?" Lizzy asked sheepishly.

"You're dragging me down baby," Ben replied.

"Oh boy," Lizzy laughed as she rolled her eyes. "You must be running out of jokes, huh?"

"I've used up all my good ones," he admitted, "but I'll come up with some great originals over the summer, you can count on that!"

"I have to admit, I'm looking forward to your new jokes!" laughed Lizzy. "So, the end of the school year is here already. It seemed like it lasted for so long, and now I can't believe it's over!"

"I know!" replied Ben. "It went pretty fast for me. But I'm so glad summer break is here! So... what are you doing over the summer, Lizzy?"

"I'm doing the summer reading program at the library, and helping with Vacation Bible School at our church. Um.... we're going camping and I get to spend two weeks at my grandparents' house in Tennessee. I can't wait! What are you doing?" she asked, as she transferred papers from her locker to her bookbag.

"Baseball, basketball camp, soccer practice and we're

renting a cabin at a lake in Michigan for a week in July."

"That sounds like fun! The vacation part of it anyways," she commented. "Not the sports! I'm not very good at sports."

"That's alright, Lizzy," replied Ben. "You're great at other things, like....multiplication, writing papers, getting friends back together, and being the best friend ever! It doesn't matter if you're not good at sports. It's better to be a great person than to be good in sports, anyways. We'll have to keep texting each other over the summer. I need someone who will laugh at my jokes!" added Ben.

"That sounds good," laughed Lizzy.

"Hey, are you going to Mrs. Weicher's homework burning party Friday night?" asked Ben.

"I sure am," replied Lizzy, "I wouldn't want to miss that! The thought of burning my old math and history homework is awesome. It should be fun!"

"Hi Lizzy. Hi Ben," said Jordan as she approached Lizzy's locker. "I can't believe the school year's over! And I didn't even blow the surprise!"

"Surprise?" asked Lizzy.

"Yeah, I almost blew it at lunchtime and told you, Lizzy!" exclaimed Jenna as she joined the trio.

"What are you talking about?" asked Lizzy anxiously.

"Your mom's working on a big surprise for us!" squealed Jordan.

"Surprise,....what kind of surprise?" asked Lizzy excitedly.

"Well," replied Jordan, "your mom called my dad to ask him if I could go to Tennessee with you over the summer and he AGREED! Can you believe it?"

"No way!" squealed Lizzy happily.

"And she called my mom to invite me to come, too!"

added Jenna happily.

"Really?" replied Lizzy loudly while she began to jump up and down. "So why didn't you tell me this morning, or right when you found out?"

"Your mom made us promise to wait until the school day was over to tell you," replied Jenna.

"The three of us on vacation together for two weeks!" shrieked Jordan. "Can you believe it?"

"That will be the best!" exclaimed Lizzy.

"I'll text you both tonight so we can start planning what to bring on the trip," replied Jenna excitedly.

"Alright," said Lizzy. "And I'll see you guys Friday night! The bonfire should be fun!"

"Yeah, it should be amazing, Lizzy!" added Jordan. "And don't forget the marshmallows!"

"You got it," Lizzy chimed as she hugged Jordan and Jenna goodbye.

"I'll see you soon!" Lizzy called as she exited the building and made her way to the parking lot to find her mom.

CHAPTER 37

Just a Work in Progress

He who began a good work in you...

Lizzy climbed into Mom's car with a big smile on her face.

"Sixth grade is OVER, Mom!" Lizzy half yelled as she climbed into the car.

"Wow, and hi to you, too," responded Mom. "How was your last day?"

"It was great," said Lizzy. "I can't believe school's out for the whole summer! And I can't believe you didn't tell me about Jordo and Jenna coming with us to Grandma and Grandpap's house!"

"Well," smiled Mom, "I wanted you to have a surprise at the end of the school day today."

"That was definitely a big surprise!" beamed Lizzy.

"Thanks, Mom! I can't believe you got Jordo's dad to actually let her go. He usually doesn't want her to go any-where over the summer break."

"It took a little coaxing on my part, and a lot of prayer," replied Mom, "but he finally agreed that it would be a good experience for Jordan."

"That's unbelievable! Jenna's never even been to Tennessee before. I can't wait!" replied Lizzy enthusiastically. "We'll have so much fun! Can we go hiking and see some more waterfalls?"

"Yes, let's plan on it!" answered Mom while smiling.

"This is going to be the best summer ever!" squealed Lizzy.

Soon Lizzy and her mom arrived at home. As Lizzy entered the house, Max greeted her with a lick on the cheek.

"Hi Max!" Lizzy exclaimed. "I get to see you every day now. We're going to have the best summer ever! Oh Mom, can Max go to Grandma and Grandpap's with us this summer? I'd hate to have him stuck in a kennel at Golden Paws for two whole weeks!"

"We're going to give it a try," replied Mom. "But he has to ride in his kennel on the trip, so he doesn't jump around and bother us while we drive."

"Yay! You get to come to Tennessee with us, Max!" crooned Lizzy happily while hugging Max.

Before getting her snack, Lizzy noticed that Max was sitting in front of his doggie biscuit drawer. He had finally learned that he could eat his snack before Lizzy had hers. Gone were the days of Lizzy chasing Max around the kitchen to retrieve her snack from his mouth, Lizzy thought.

After giving Max a doggie treat, Lizzy began thinking about which activity she would like to do on her first free evening. She had a book she couldn't wait to read, a paint by number oil picture to start, and an adventure movie to watch. She decided to do all three on her first free evening.

Mom had declared it snack night, which Lizzy always loved. She could help herself to any snacks for dinner, as long as some of them were healthy. With the warmer weather back again, she was getting especially hungry for ice cream! After some reading and painting, she decided on her snack. She went into the kitchen and made herself some ants on a log with celery, creamy peanut butter, and raisins. After putting them on a large plate, she added some bbq potato chips, an orange, some peanuts and a giant homemade chocolate chip cookie sitting in a big bowl of ice cream. As she sat at the table to eat, Max quickly ran to the table and grabbed her cookie, galloping into the hallway with it in his mouth.

"No, Max!" yelled Lizzy. "Mom! He's got my cookie!"

Lizzy and Mom were able to corner Max in the kitchen, and once again Lizzy had to pry the cookie out of his mouth.

"I guess this is going to take a little more work," Lizzy groaned as she tossed the crumbled cookie into the trash can. "Oh well, we have all summer long to work on your manners, Max. I'll bet that by the end of the summer you'll be the best dog ever!"

As Lizzy gave Max a hug, he lowered his head and looked her in the eyes as if to say I'm sorry.

"I forgive you, Max," Lizzy said while hugging him. "I guess we're all just a work in progress. But no matter how many times you swipe my snack, I'll still love you."

Lizzy thoroughly enjoyed her first night of summer break. She spent a lot of time with Max and was determined to work hard on training him over the summer.

Eventually, it was getting late and Lizzy decided to head to bed. Dad came to Lizzy's room to tell her goodnight.

"Hey, Kiddo, are you ready for bed?" asked Dad.

"Yep, I'm tired," stated Lizzy.

"Are you glad the school year's over?" Dad asked thoughtfully.

"Am I ever!" Lizzy exclaimed.

"I'm sure you'll enjoy summer break," said Dad. "I know you had a challenging school year, but I'm hoping next year will be better for you. Your mom and I watched you grow and mature. We were impressed with the compassion you showed toward Kaylee, and you modeled some wonderful character traits in the process. You know, Honey, life is a process of trial and error. You try different things and learn what you're good at, and what you're not so good at. Even though sports may not be your thing…"

"You got that right!" interrupted Lizzy.

"God has given all of us gifts and talents. It's just a matter of figuring out those gifts and abilities that He's given to you that make you special. I hope you don't get discouraged when you don't succeed at something, Kiddo. As you get older, you'll find those things that you're good at and life will get easier. You'll discover more and more things that you can do well."

"I hope so," added Lizzy. "Sometimes I feel like I can't do anything right!"

"Well, just be patient," encouraged Dad. "God's got it all under control and He loves you very much. He wants what's best for you, even though there are times when it doesn't feel like it. So,… what was the most important thing you learned during the school year?"

"I learned…," Lizzy replied thoughtfully, "that sometimes people are mean because they're unhappy. And if they pick on you, it's better to forgive them, and pray for them. Because, if you get mad and try to get even with them, then you become mean just like they are. But…you can't let them walk all over you either. So, if you need to tell an adult, that's okay. Oh, I also want to leave a good legacy for others."

"That's great, I'm very proud of you, Lizzy," replied Dad. "I think you've become very wise. I hope you enjoy your much deserved summer vacation. You've worked very hard this year in school! Have a good night's sleep, Honey. I love you."

"Goodnight, Dad, I love you, too," replied Lizzy as she pulled the fresh smelling bed sheet up under her chin. Before Lizzy drifted off to sleep, she prayed:

"Dear Lord, thanks for letting me make it through another school year. Thanks for my family, and for summer vacation. Please help Jordo, Jenna and Kaylee to have a good summer, too. Help me to discover those talents that you've given me; they have to be in here SOMEWHERE! And help me to leave a good legacy...and thanks also for all of the different flavors of ice cream! Yum! Amen."

"For I know the plans I have for you declares the Lord, plans to prosper you and not to harm you, plans to give you hope and a future." Joshua 29:11

THE END

To contact the author, you may reach her at:

sgerken60@gmail.com

Made in the USA
Middletown, DE
17 February 2022

61151267R00078